570

A WREATH OF
CHERRY BLOSSOM

David Chan came to Kyoto to find a man who had vanished, and immediately found himself pitted against the *YAKUSA*, the notorious 'Mafia of Japan.' It seemed that there were any number of people interested in finding the enigmatic Tony Fallon, but no one seemed to know why. Where was he? Was he alive? The search takes Chan from Kyoto to Osaka, to Mount Nantai and the Inland Sea, and death lurks behind the inscrutable mask of every smile.

CHARLES LEADER

A WREATH OF CHERRY BLOSSOM

Complete and Unabridged

LINFORD
Leicester

First published in Great Britain

First Linford Edition
published 1996

British Library CIP Data

Leader, Charles, *1938*–
   A wreath of cherry blossom.—Large print ed.—
Linford mystery library
1. English fiction—20th century
I. Title
823.9′14 [F]

ISBN 0–7089–7933–5

Published by
F. A. Thorpe (Publishing) Ltd.
Anstey, Leicestershire

Set by Words & Graphics Ltd.
Anstey, Leicestershire
Printed and bound in Great Britain by
T. J. Press (Padstow) Ltd., Padstow, Cornwall

This book is printed on acid-free paper

1

THERE is a dark Japan beneath the polite smiles and the bright sprays of cherry blossom, and searching for a man named Tony Fallon was a dangerous occupation. I began to appreciate both those facts when the girl in the blue silk *kimono* straightened up from her deep bow and exposed the little black automatic she had removed from her flowing sleeve. Her smile was charming, tiny but perfect white teeth set in rich red lips that were the essence of sweetness itself. Her hand was slim and dainty, as though a big gun would have been too heavy for her, but she held the snub-nosed 0.32 steadily enough.

From a distance of three feet she would have to be blind or hysterical to miss and even a small calibre bullet hole can be fatal. Consequently I did nothing dramatic.

It was only twenty-four hours since I had arrived in Kyoto, once the ancient capital and now the fifth largest city in Japan. The month was April and the afternoon sun was sufficiently warm for me to stroll with my jacket over my arm. The sky was cloudless turquoise behind the dark green, pine-clothed hills that embraced the city and its shrines. Here in the temple gardens the distant traffic sound was muted and birds sang. Golden carp splashed lazily in the blue-grey lake that was dotted with miniature islands of rocks and dwarf pines. The cherry blossom made red and white, spring-scented canopies and curtains over the shaded paths. It was all very peaceful and through the trees I could see the graceful grey slope of a roof and the gold-leafed walls of the Kinkaku-Ji, once the luxurious villa of the third *Shogun* but now more widely known as the golden pavilion.

It was there that I had arranged to meet Sharon Vale, the American girl who had hired me to find Tony Fallon, and until this moment there had been no thought in my mind that I might fail to make the rendezvous.

I had stopped walking when I turned the corner to find the young Japanese couple blocking my path. The girl was perhaps twenty. Her shining black hair was piled high, elegantly coiffured and secured with long, jewelled pins. The broad waist sash that went with the blue *kimono* was pure and spotless white, almost dazzling to the eye, and she wore white slippers on her feet.

She had inclined her head humbly, and I had assumed that the gesture was one of courtesy, an expression of Japanese manners in the traditional fashion. Now, as she lifted her face again, I saw that there was no humility in her laughing eyes, and there was nothing courteous about the gun.

My Chinese father had once said that discretion was a virtue equal to valour — or perhaps it was something that I had learned from my English mother. However, the thought came into my mind and seemed a suitable maxim for the moment. I had paused in mid-stride and I remained carefully motionless.

The young man moved up beside his charming companion. I judged his age to be in the middle twenties and he was a few inches taller than the average Japanese. He had the smooth movement of a man confident of his own strength and command of the situation. His dark oblique eyes gleamed with a malicious humour and there was a half smile on his lips. He wore a smart black suit, gloss-polished black shoes, and a white polo-neck shirt.

"You look surprised, Mister Chan?" His voice held a slight hiss that was not unduly sinister. Hissing is a national characteristic with the Japanese, especially with an unfamiliar language.

"I am surprised," I admitted. Even in my business it is rare to stumble upon complete strangers brandishing

4

lethal weapons. "Who are you? And why does your friend find it necessary to point a gun?"

"My name is Shino," he said with the false modesty that signifies pride. "My friend is named Kukiko."

"And what do you want?"

"Some English conversation."

Shino laughed at his own joke. I had been long enough in Japan to realize that every student was desperately hungry for English conversation. English was the language of business and exports and their hopeful passport to the higher echelons of the *Zaibatsu*, the giant commercial empires that had re-emerged to dominate the economic miracle that was modern Japan. Shino knew that any visitor quickly became familiar with the request, but it was obvious that he was no student. He had the air of a man who had already made his mark upon the world, but his was not the world of high school or university, or even the advanced rat-race of commerce. Besides, he didn't wear spectacles, which were the oriental badge of the studious.

"But not here," he qualified. "We must ask you to walk with us."

He moved up on my left side, turned and indicated the path ahead with a polite wave of his hand. The girl stepped up on my right, turned so that her shoulder brushed my arm, and smiled again as her right hand and the automatic disappeared into her wide sleeve. It was all very refined, as though we had just become friends, and because the hidden automatic was still levelled at my heart I allowed them to lead me forward.

Shino set the pace, a casual stroll. Kukiko tripped delicately by my side, the *kimono* forcing her to take quick, tiny steps. She glanced at me sideways through black, slanted eyes and her arms were ostensibly folded in the manner of a well-bred young Japanese lady. A small party of tourists returning from the cultural shrine passed us by without noticing anything amiss.

We turned off the main path and skirted the lake. The golden pavilion cast a clear reflection in the still water, a three-storied gem of classical Japanese architecture with two tiers of slanting roofs and a golden phoenix settling on the apex. The surrounding gardens were a gentle joy to behold, designed by Zen Buddhists who had sought to achieve their essential harmony of God and Nature. It was very quiet and restful, as though this was indeed a heavenly oasis in a mad world, which made my own predicament seem even more bizarre and unbelievable.

The lake passed from view behind a screen of pine trees and then Shino indicated another fork in the path. A few moments later another pavilion appeared, nestling half-hidden among the pines. This was a simple one-storey structure with a railed verandah. As we approached Shino made another move of his hand, a polite invitation for me to ascend ahead of him.

I climbed the three short steps to

the wooden verandah. Kukiko was no longer on my immediate right and that meant she would now have to draw the gun from her sleeve and aim before she could fire. I wondered how fast and how accurate she might be? And whether any initiative on my part would be worth the risk.

Shino stepped up behind me. "Please Mister Chan, go into the pavilion."

I glanced back at him. I saw that Kukiko had not allowed him to block her line of fire. Instead she had moved along the outside of the verandah at ground level and was gazing up at me with watchful eyes. She looked too confident so I did as I was told.

Shino was taking no chances either. Inside the pavilion two men were waiting in the shadows. They were two very solid men, not exceptionally tall but heavy. They wore dark, double-breasted pin-stripe suits with white polo-neck shirts, which made them look like pugilists dressed up as businessmen. They had dull, unimpressive faces which were not exactly brimming over with intelligence. However, one of them held a gun, an 8mm Japanese Nambu that looked rather like a Luger and was slightly larger than Kukiko's little 0.32, and he did look bright enough to know how to pull the trigger.

"These are my friends," Shino said politely.

He didn't bother to name them and so I assumed that they were of less worth and even more humble origins than he pretended to be himself. For my own convenience I mentally christened them with the first names that came to mind, Tweedledumshi and Tweedledishi, the latter being the one with the gun.

Tweedledumshi smiled at me and showed a couple of broken teeth, and I decided that he probably worked as a bouncer in a low quality geisha-house in his spare time. From his pocket he took a large pair of dark glasses which he fixed on to my face. They were the close-fitting type that gave total protection from the sun and they had been painted black on the inside. While wearing them I was neatly and unobtrusively made blind.

I felt Shino take my arm and heard him chuckle. "Now we take another walk, Mister Chan, a little further this time."

He turned me round and we left the pavilion. I heard the floorboards creak briefly as the two heavyweights followed. At the bottom of the steps Kukiko took my other arm and began chattering gaily in Japanese. Shino occasionally answered her as we strolled back through the gardens, and to any casual observer it must have seemed that all three of us were indulged in amiable conversation. Only the scuff of shoes on gravel reminded me that our new friends were still close behind.

After a few minutes the gravel path ended and I sensed a hard pavement beneath my feet. The traffic sounds were closer and I heard a car swish past, evidence that we had left the temple grounds. Shino stopped me for a moment.

"There is a car in front of you. Please get inside."

I ducked my head carefully and found the car. I got in and Shino joined me. The door opened on the far side and one of the heavyweights got in. It was a tight squeeze with three of us in the back. I guessed that the second heavyweight was driving and that Kukiko had the front passenger seat. Doors slammed and the engine started. The car moved forward.

"Is this where we begin our English conversation?" I asked hopefully.

"When we reach our destination." Shino was brief.

"Which is where?"

"You will see — or rather you will not see." Shino chuckled. He found all his own jokes funny.

We became silent. I could hear nothing but traffic sounds. I tried moving my eyebrows to create a side gap where the dark glasses fitted close to my temples. Shino was obviously watching for he used two fingers to press the glasses more firmly over my eyes. There wasn't much more that I could do except to endure the ride.

I had time to think, to contemplate on the doubtful wisdom of operating alone in a strange city. I had established the David Chan Detective Agency in Hong Kong, where it ran very smoothly with the aid of two beautiful and intelligent young women, my partners, Belinda Carrington and Tracey Ryan. At this moment Tracey was employed as a receptionist in a Hong Kong clinic where small but frequent thefts of drugs had occurred. The agency had been hired to find the thief. That meant that I had been obliged to leave Belinda in charge of the agency office while I accompanied our client to Japan. It was our modest claim that we could operate capably anywhere in South East Asia and the Orient, excluding Communist China.

Now I began to wonder if our

claim had not been modest enough. I had advised our client to go direct to a Japanese agency, recommending Ken Kenichi in Tokyo to whom we usually assigned any Japanese business that came our way. However, our own reputation had become more inflated than I had realized. Sharon Vale had insisted that she did not want to take her troubles to a Japanese detective who would only have a limited knowledge of English, she had wanted the personal services of David Chan.

I had been flattered, and although I would have to use Kenichi to some extent anyway there had been no other demands on my time. Only now did I begin to realize that finding Tony Fallon might not be such a simple piece of routine detection work. And now I did not have Belinda and Tracey to feed me with good advice, or to scrape me out of trouble when I neglected to take it.

While those thoughts idled in my mind the car was making a large

number of twists and turns as it moved
erratically through the Kyoto traffic.
Every few seconds it either accelerated,
braked, swerved, or bumped over the
unmistakable streetcar lines. I didn't try
to count the number of turns, or time
the intervals between each, because the
driver was obviously going out of his
way to mislead me.

After half an hour the car stopped
and I was ushered out on to the
pavement. I listened but all that I could
hear was the movements of my four
companions. There were no pedestrian
voices and no traffic sounds. We were
still in Kyoto but clearly in one of the
quieter suburbs. Shino took my arm
again, and Kukiko sweetly suggested
that we walk.

We walked. It was a gentle uphill
slope and the hard pavement gave way
to a gravel path after the first few steps.
I could now hear a bird singing again
and the air was clean with the scent
of pines. I guessed we were in another
temple garden, although it was possible

they had tried to deceive me by coming full circle back to our starting point.

Shino stopped me and warned me of more steps. I counted four and then I was on the wooden flooring of another verandah. The extra step told me that it wasn't the same one. We walked a few more paces and then Shino halted me again.

"We go inside. Please take off your shoes."

I did as he asked. In Japan it is a cardinal sin to wear outdoor shoes inside a temple or the home. In fact there are elaborate shoe-changing rituals to cover anywhere that anyone could conceivably set their feet. It was a Japanese peculiarity that I was beginning to acknowledge, but it was strange to find the criminal fraternity treating the rules with same respect. Kidnapping was presumably okay, but the shoe-changing law was inviolate.

We went inside and I felt *tatami*, the close-woven straw matting that the Japanese use for carpeting, under my stockinged feet. I sensed that we were in a corridor, for the pine scent and the bird song were shut out and I had the feeling of being narrowly enclosed. I heard a brief murmur of low voices, as though we had passed an open door, but then all was hushed again. A floorboard creaked beneath my foot and two steps later the sound was repeated. I remembered that the wily old *Shoguns* had deliberately installed loose floorboards in their pavilions and palaces to give advance warning of approaching assassins. They had lived in dangerous times. In those terms I wondered if the world had made any progress?

We turned two corners in the long, rambling corridor, and then we stopped. Shino released my arm and removed the dark glasses from my eyes.

We were standing in a low-ceiling room with polished wood-panelled walls. *Tatami* covered the floor. It was not a large room and we were facing two decorated screens that concealed the far end. The paintings on the screens were landscapes in the fifteenth century style, plumes of water falling through wreathes of mist and those peculiar twisted trees clinging to rocky hillsides.

The two heavyweights had moved up on either side of Shino and Kukiko so that we now stood in a line, all gazing attentively at the screens. There was an air of expectancy so I contented myself with waiting. The paintings, etched in green and white on a faded yellow background, were pleasing to the eye, and it was a full minute before a figure emerged from between the screens.

He was an impressive figure, made tall by the pointed white head-dress that flowed into a wide cape behind him. He wore heavy purple silk robes and a splendid red and white shoulder sash that was secured with tasselled white cords. His face was heavily jowled with deep wrinkles at the corners of his eyes. It was a calm face but unsmiling, a face with more than religious authority. From his regalia I recognized that he was a Buddhist Grand Monk.

Shino and Kukiko and the two heavyweights all bowed deeply. The Grand Monk commanded reverence and no doubt I was expected to do the same. However, I was becoming bored with doing exactly what was expected, and now that they all had their faces level with their knees I had an opportunity that was too good to miss. With my left hand I gave Shino a violent push that tumbled him off balance to collide with Tweedledumshi. In the same moment I used my right hand to shove Kukiko equally rudely against Tweedledishi. Then I spun on my heel and raced back down the corridor.

I heard Shino yelling angrily behind me but I didn't look back. I was anxious to get around the first corner before anyone could fire a shot. I made it and put on another spurt down the next stretch of corridor. I

18

passed an open doorway on my left and saw a brief glimpse of a temple interior with a gilded Buddha image and incense burning in bronze offering bowls. I was tempted to seek escape that way but while my attention was momentarily distracted a *kendo* stave lashed out from a second doorway on my right and neatly cut my legs from under me.

I fell heavily and felt for a moment as though my leg was broken. The long wooden pole had cracked across my shinbone and the pain was excruciating. Dimly, through the sudden mist of tears, I saw the gross, squat figure who had checked my flight. He waddled into the corridor with a grin like a besotted gorilla and laughed. It was a shrill, cackling sound, something like a neighing horse with laryngitis.

He wore a judo jacket and trousers and as he leaned over me I saw thick rolls of obscene fat through the loose folds. He wrapped monstrous arms around me and lifted me up. I couldn't breathe and felt as though my ribs must collapse under the terrible pressure of his embrace.

Then I heard Shino's chuckle behind me. My captor turned me round to face him.

"Please, Mister Chan, it will be best if you do not struggle." Shino looked happy as he gave me the benefit of his advice. "Toji is a *sumo* wrestler and he is very strong. If he becomes upset he could easily crush you to a pulp."

2

NEVER look a gift buffalo in the mouth, my father had once said, and so my decision to escape had been an impulse generated by what had seemed a favourable moment. Now that it had failed I could only accept that failure philosophically. I was curious to know who these people were and why they had kidnapped me, and eventually I would have come back to find out. I could pretend that it didn't really matter whether I learned the answers now or later, on their terms or my own. Or, to put it more honestly, my shinbone hurt so abominably that I knew I wouldn't be capable of running anywhere for the next ten minutes anyway.

"I won't struggle," I promised Shino with the minimal gasps of breath that I could get up from my compressed lungs.

Tweedledishi had come puffing up with his Nambu waving in his hand and so Shino spoke briefly in Japanese. Reluctantly Toji released me and stepped back. His bulging moon face had a hangdog expression, as though he had just been robbed of a new-found bone.

They escorted me back into the presence. The Grand Monk had not moved and regarded me with the same stone-faced calm. His hands were crossed patiently in front of him and I noticed that on one finger he wore a jewelled ring.

Kukiko was patting her glossy hair to make sure that nothing was out of place and she looked the most offended of all. Her face was an expression of pained and righteous anger.

Shino kept a firm grip on my arm and addressed a spate of respectful Japanese to the Grand Monk. I understood nothing and could only wait. When Shino finished the senior man turned his face towards me. There were deep creases from his nose to the sides of his mouth which gave him a cruel look as they became shadowed. His eyes were hard in their narrow slits and I reflected that he might have made a better warlord than a priest.

"I bid you welcome, Mister Chan," he said carefully. "Mister Shino and Miss Kukiko have already been introduced. You may address me as Mister Morita. I understand that you do not speak Japanese. I do not speak Chinese. Therefore our conversations will be in English, which I believe is a mutual language."

I nodded. "Perhaps you will begin by explaining why I have been brought here?" I suggested politely.

There was silence. Morita simply stared at me.

"You will begin by telling us everything you know about the American Tony Fallon?" Shino countered. His tone and the glint in his eye made it plain that I had not been invited here to ask the questions, merely to answer them.

"I know nothing about him, or at least very little. He is missing and I am trying to find him."

"Why? Is he a friend of yours?"

"No."

"Then why?"

I ignored him and looked back to the Grand Monk.

"I thought your priesthood only sought Enlightenment. Why are you so interested in Tony Fallon?"

"Mister Chan!" Shino snapped my name and made it a warning. Obviously he was in charge of the interrogation. Perhaps it was all beneath the dignity of Mister Morita, who seemed to have nothing more to say now that he had formally introduced himself. However, no matter how well he did his facial imitation of a stone wall, he was still an interested party, and still the final pinnacle of authority.

"I think you should realize that we are fully aware of all your movements since your arrival in Kyoto yesterday afternoon." Shino captured my attention again and his tight smile registered satisfaction. "You came here with an American woman and booked adjoining rooms at the Kyoto Tower Hotel. This morning you hired a car and then visited a Japanese-style hotel, the *Yushimaso Ryokan* near Kitayama-Dori Avenue in the north eastern part of Kyoto. There you asked questions of the manager about Tony Fallon. This afternoon you drove to Osaka, to the Koga car factory, where you asked for an interview with the chairman of the company, a man named Mister Shinjira. You were there for an hour, asking questions about Tony Fallon. Then you returned to Kyoto, and Kinkaku-Ji temple where we found you."

His smile suggested that I was an object to be pitied and he continued; "You see, Mister Chan, we already know many things about you. Therefore it is pointless for you to conceal any further information."

"I have nothing to conceal," I said

blandly. "I have admitted that I am trying to find a man who has apparently disappeared, but so far I have not been successful. It would seem that perhaps you are in a better position to help me than I am to assist you. After all, Japan is your country, and Kyoto is your city." I paused. "Where is Tony Fallon?"

I glanced at Mister Morita but his face was unchanged. Shino was getting nastier every minute.

"Do not play games with us, Mister Chan. We wish to know why you have come here to ask questions about this man. If he is not your friend, then why are you concerned to find him?"

I was thoughtful for a moment. "Perhaps I can say that he is the friend of a friend?"

"What does that mean?" Shino shouted with exasperation.

I decided that telling the truth could hardly be detrimental to my position and might even prompt some return cooperation. At this stage I couldn't see that there was anything to lose.

"I am a private detective," I explained quietly. "I have an agency in Hong Kong. I was approached there by a client who subsequently engaged me to find Tony Fallon. That is the job I am trying to do."

Shino glared at me doubtfully. "What were you told about this man?"

"He is an American from Detroit. He is aged about thirty-five. He is employed by an American company that imports a small number of Japanese cars into the United States. He makes frequent visits to Tokyo and Osaka to place orders with Japanese manufacturers. His last visit was made three weeks ago, and his return is now two weeks overdue. Nothing has been heard from him, by his family, his firm, or his friends, since he arrived in Japan."

There was silence. Shino continued to glare at me and did not appear to be any way appeased by my compliance. Tweedledumshi shifted uncomfortably from one foot to the other. Toji coughed hoarsely. Somewhere, very deep and muted within the temple I could hear the chanting of prayers.

"This girl who is with you at the hotel!" Shino snapped abruptly. "Who is she?"

"She is my secretary." I kept a bland face and lied boldly. If they knew that Sharon Vale was my client they could be tempted to kidnap and interrogate her too. As my secretary she could not reasonably be expected to know any more than I knew myself.

Shino was not entirely fooled. "Who engaged you to search for Tony Fallon?" he demanded.

"His American employers," I lied again. "Morrison and Brooks, Automobile Imports of Detroit, Michigan. A senior partner in the firm cabled my office in Hong Kong and requested that I make some enquiries after their missing representative."

Shino looked frustrated, but he made an effort to show that he had patience. "Mister Chan, let us assume for a moment that you are telling the truth, that you are a private detective searching for a man who is not personally known to you and whom you have never met. You arrived in Tokyo. What led you here to Kyoto and the *Yushimaso Ryokan*?"

"I succeeded in finding the *ryokan* where Fallon stayed in Tokyo." That was half a lie because Ken Kenichi had located it for me, but I saw no reason for bringing his name to their attention. I continued: "Fallon had spoken of his intention to travel on to Kyoto, and so the manager of the Tokyo *ryokan* had recommended the *Yushimaso Ryokan*. It was a simple trail to follow."

"Why did you visit the Koga car company?"

"Because Fallon mentioned to the manager of the *Yushimaso* that he had business with Koga cars. When I talked to Mister Shinjira this afternoon he told me that he and Fallon had discussed shipping arrangements and delivery dates for an order of twenty of the new model Koga 1000 saloons. This was ten days ago. Fallon should have returned the following day to sign the agreement, but he didn't show up. He left the *Yushimaso Ryokan* the same evening, dressed for a social evening, but he didn't return. No one has seen him since."

"So what will you do now?"

"I haven't decided. The trail runs to a dead end."

"You have told us nothing we do not know already."

I smiled. "I cannot tell you anything I do not know myself."

"Mister Chan, you are a liar!" Shino was infuriated by my smile. "I do not believe you are a private detective. I believe you *are* a Chinese spy!"

It was an interesting accusation and I gave him my carefully practised look of curious innocence. "Why should you believe that?"

"Shino." The word of warning came from the Grand Monk and he made a slight negative move of his hand. It was his first word and his first move for the past fifteen minutes and I hoped that it was a good sign. He studied my face for another minute and then decided that the damage was done.

"Well, Mister Chan," he said softly. "Are you an agent for the communist Chinese?"

"No." I paused. "Are you?"

The heavy jowls wobbled slightly, as though the buried muscles might have twitched with wry amusement, but his eyes remained the same.

"No, Mister Chan," he said positively. He studied my face again, trying to undermine my composure with his stare. "But you are Chinese?"

"Eurasian," I corrected politely. I had the best streams of both Chinese and English blood in my veins and I didn't care who knew it.

"I ask you one more time." His voice was still soft and his eyes did not blink. "Where is Tony Fallon?"

I could only give him the same answer. "I don't know."

"Perhaps we should let Toji play with him," Shino suggested.

Morita frowned and shook his head. He glanced at the huge *sumo* wrestler as though acknowledging his presence for the first time and made a sign of dismissal. Toji looked disappointed but he bowed low to conceal his expression in an act of reverence. Then he backed out into the corridor behind us.

Morita looked back at Shino and the two heavyweights and made another sign. Then he turned and walked slowly through the gap between the painted screens. Shino followed him with Tweedledumshi and Tweedledishi dutifully bringing up the rear.

Only Kukimo remained.

"What happens now?" I asked her.

"The Grand Monk must think," she replied calmly. "Then perhaps he will discuss his thoughts with Shino. We must wait."

I guessed that Toji would be blocking

the corridor and that the two heavy-weights would be lurking beyond the screens. There were no other exits so I decided that she was right. My leg still throbbed and I flexed it briefly.

"You are hurt!" Kukiko expressed concern, but was quick to add that it was my own fault. "It was foolish of you to run away, and it was very bad manners in front of Mister Morita."

"I apologize, but it is not exactly courteous to kidnap people," I defended myself humbly.

"But you were not kidnapped. Why do you use such a word? You were simply requested to accompany us."

I decided not to split hairs. It would be too tedious to remind her of the gun that was still tucked away inside her *kimono*.

She was silent for a moment and then she became solicitous again.

"Perhaps it is best if you sit down. You can rest your leg."

She took my arm and we sat down together on the tatami. Kukiko tucked her legs behind her and smoothed down the blue silk of her *kimono*. She smiled at me and again her smile was soft and sweet. I was a stranger but she seemed very sure of herself in my company, and I wondered if she had been trained as a geisha. She leaned towards me and gently ran her hand down my leg from the knee.

"There is nothing broken. I think it can only be bruised."

I nodded polite agreement. Obviously I would not have remained standing for so long if the bone had been broken, but there was no value in rudeness for its own sake. She continued to smile and stroke my leg.

"Mister Chan, why do you not tell the truth to Mister Morita? Everything would then be so much more pleasant."

"I have already told the truth to Mister Morita."

"But I do not think that you have told all the truth. Neither does Shino. Neither does Mister Morita. If you are wholly honest then no harm will come to you." It was a discreetly veiled threat. "Mister Morita is a very good man."

"Who is Mister Morita?"

"Mister Morita is a Buddhist Grand Monk." She looked surprised at my ignorance.

"What else is he?"

"I do not understand."

"Why does he associate with criminals?"

She looked shocked. "What do you mean?"

"I mean Shino and Toji, and Shino's friends." I could have added her own name but I was being tactful.

"But they are not criminals."

"They are certainly not monks."

Her face expressed pain and she changed the subject. "Mister Chan, I believe you are involved in a business that you do not wholly understand. I definitely advise you to tell us everything you know, and then return to Hong Kong."

"And what of Tony Fallon, the man

I am supposed to find? And why is he so important to Shino and Mister Morita?"

Kukiko stopped stroking my leg and folded her hands in her lap. Her smile faded.

"Mister Chan," she stressed plaintively. "I am trying to help you."

She stood up and walked away as far as the confines of the room would permit. I shrugged my shoulders and finished rubbing my own leg. Half a minute passed and then there was the rustle of silk robes on the *tatami*. The Grand Monk and Shino reappeared from between the screens. I stood up to face them.

Morita glanced briefly at the girl. Kukiko inclined her head with a sad, negative movement, which conveyed the fact that she had been unable to discover anything useful in their absence.

Morita frowned and then his eyes fixed on mine.

"Perhaps it was a mistake to bring

36

you here, Mister Chan. It would seem that you know nothing that is helpful. You will leave this place now and we shall not meet again."

"You mean I am free to go?"

"Not quite. I am afraid that Shino and his friends must accompany you."

He made a slight bow and then returned through the screens. He must have included a sign to Kukiko for she immediately followed. Either she had no desire to look back or she didn't dare, she hurried with her head bowed and her arms folded. The two heavyweights had now joined Shino and all three of them favoured me with toothy, malicious smiles.

Tweedledishi pointed his Nambu automatic and Tweedledumshi took out his specially prepared dark glasses and fitted them over my eyes. I was blind again and they led me out of the building.

We stopped to collect our shoes and then returned to the car. Once again I was squashed into the back seat between Shino and Tweedledishi, while Tweedledumshi took the wheel. They were taking no chances but this time they drove direct to our next destination. The car made only three turns. After that I felt no more streetcar lines and our speed increased, a good indication that we were leaving the city. I knew then that I was being taken for a ride in the American gangster style. The Japanese are born imitators in everything.

When the car stopped I was ordered out. I could feel cool night air on my face. I judged that it was over two hours since I had first encountered Shino and Kukiko on the path to the Kinkaku-Ji, so now the sun had gone down. It was early Spring and the days were still short. Perhaps life was shorter, the thought made me feel suddenly cold.

"This way, Mister Chan." Shino jabbed a gun barrel in my ribs and I realized that now he was also armed. Probably he had carried the gun all the time, but only now found it necessary to use it.

They steered me across the grass verge at the roadside and then helped me to step over a low wire fence. Beyond was a steep, grass hillside sloping downward. Here I slipped a couple of times but they were keeping a tight grip on me now to ensure that I didn't fall. At the bottom of the slope they warned me of another wire fence.

Beyond the second fence the ground was level again and they marched me more briskly. There was gravel under my feet and suddenly I kicked against solid steel. I stopped with a curse.

"Step over it, Mister Chan." The hiss had crept back into Shino's voice and this time he did sound sinister.

I stepped over the obstacle, feeling carefully with my feet. Then we stopped, and Tweedledumshi took the black-painted glasses from my eyes.

I saw that I was standing in the middle of a railway track that ran through a deep cut between high earth banks. The steel lines gleamed like polished silver in the starlight.

"The New Tokaido Line," Shino informed me proudly. "It carries the fastest train in the world, the bullet express from Tokyo to Osaka at one-hundred-and-twenty-six miles per hour. In Japan the trains are always on time, and the bullet train is due in precisely one minute."

The two heavyweights were grinning and Shino continued:

"In Japan there are many suicides, and many people choose to throw themselves under the bullet express. This is a favourite spot and the police are accustomed to finding bodies. Another one will not make them curious, for usually the victims are too badly damaged for recognition."

As he spoke I heard the thunder of the approaching train. I looked up and saw the double white spotlights hurtling towards me, and then I sensed a movement from behind. I started to spin round but I was too late. It may have been a cosh or it may have been the butt of the Nambu automatic, but something solid smashed at the base of my skull and knocked me senseless across the track.

3

I WAS lucky. I had realized a split second too slowly how they intended to murder me, but the fact that I had started to turn my head meant that the blow had not landed true to its author's aim. It was a glancing blow that tumbled me unconscious for only a fleeting moment of time, perhaps enough time to have snapped my fingers, or to have blinked twice.

Even so it was almost enough to see the end of me. The bullet express was bearing down upon me at the rate of two miles per minute like a streamlined rocket. The stabbing glare of the twin headlights blazed fiercely above my head as my senses swam back, making the night twice as brilliant as day. I was blinded by the dazzle and deafened by the monstrous roar of power. The numbed compartments of my brain were still too badly shaken for any rational thought, but my instinct for survival was activated by terror alone. I rolled to my left and my shoulder hit heavily against the steel railway line. I heaved myself up and over the rail. For a brief moment my body was balanced on the narrow altar of steel, a sacrificial offering to the descending wheeled knives. Then I dropped to safety and the super express streaked past in a mighty avalanche of speed blur and ear-shattering sound.

I continued to roll desperately away, terrified that I might still be sucked back under the flashing wheels by the rushing slipstream of displaced air. A hurricane of wind beat at my back and shoulders and the carriage windows made a flashing tracer fire of lights that prolonged my blindness.

Then abruptly it was over and the blue and white monster had disappeared down the track.

I was alive but for a few moments

I was not sure. My whole body was soaked in a muck sweat and every muscle I owned felt like mashed jelly. My face stung with laceration from the tiny stones that had been thrown up by the slipstream, and my stomach wanted to be sick. My head was a swollen balloon, inflated with pain and that mind-exploding roar of sound that was still echoing in my ears.

My hearing came back and faintly I heard the sound of a car departing on the road above. I opened my eyes and saw that I was face down with my fingers dug deep into the black dirt in front of me. I pushed myself up into a sitting position and was relieved to find that all my limbs were intact. I discovered later that a corner of my jacket had been chopped off.

I felt gently at the back of my head, using the tips of my fingers. There was a bump that was very tender, but no stickiness that would have meant blood, and no indentation that would have meant a broken skull.

My thought processes were clear now and I decided that I had suffered no serious damage.

I got to my feet. I was shaky but I didn't collapse. I let the night wind cool my face and breathed deeply to let the night air settle my stomach.

There was no sign of Shino and his friends, and I guessed that it was their car I had heard moving away. Either through confidence or caution they had decided not to linger. I was glad of that, because although I wanted to meet up with Shino again I didn't want it to be right now. I needed a few hours recovery time.

I brushed myself down and cleaned up my face with a handkerchief. Then I climbed up the grass bank to regain the road. The car sound had faded to my left so I guessed that Kyoto lay in that direction. I began to walk along the roadside.

Five minutes and a dozen cars went past before I succeeded in stopping a red Toyota saloon. The driver was an obliging little man who seemed only too happy to give me a ride, and as he spoke only Japanese I was spared the necessity of any contrived explanations. He drove fast through a range of dark hills and soon we were descending into the lights of Kyoto. He dropped me outside the Kyoto Tower Hotel and then sped on his way with a wave and a cheerful *sayonara*.

It was nice to know that the Japanese were not all villains.

★ ★ ★

I should have gone straight to my room to clean up, but I didn't. I was worried about Sharon Vale. My client was a slim young woman in her early twenties, a blue-eyed blonde with long hair that fell in curling waves to her shoulders. Her expression was often one of youthful innocence, and in our conversations she often appeared confused and uncertain. She radiated a need for a strong, level-headed male.

Belinda had warned me that Sharon was not necessarily as helpless as she seemed, and that I could be a sucker falling for an act. However, Belinda is frequently sceptical of her own sex, and as she is partially in love with me I considered that she could be biased.

I knocked on Sharon's door and waited. Half a minute passed with no sound and I began to feel that my worst fears would be confirmed. I reached for the door handle, but then the door opened. Sharon gazed at me with relief, her blue eyes very wide. She wore a black skirt and a cherry red jumper with a turtle neck and a double string of white beads. She had obviously been keyed up, because now she visibly relaxed.

"David, I've been so worried about you. I waited for hours in the temple garden but you never turned up. We've both been wondering where you could possibly be?"

The *we* warned me that she was not alone. I glanced over her shoulder and saw a man rising from a chair. His dark suit looked expensive but crumpled, and in any case no material would ever drape smartly on his short, fat body. He wore a white collar and a conservative tie of blue and dark blue stripes. His belted raincoat and a dark felt hat were laid over another chair. He was aged about fifty. He had a plump face with spectacles and scrubbing-brush bristles of stiff grey hair.

"David, this is Inspector Yamamoto," Sharon said quickly.

"Mister David Chan, I am honoured to meet you."

Yamamoto added a smile to the words and offered me his hand. He didn't bow. His fingers were pudgy and inelegant, but there was an unexpected strength in his grip. Also he was observant, his eyes examined me shrewdly.

"Have you been in an accident?"

"A small one," I admitted. "A fall."

"Do you require medical attention?"

"No, just a drink." I returned his

smile and moved to help myself from the bottle of scotch that stood with glasses and a soda syphon on the table. "Will you join me?"

"No." He was apologetic. "I drink only *saki*."

"I'll call down for a bottle." Sharon moved towards the telephone but Yamamoto stopped her with a wave of his hand.

"It is not necessary."

Sharon stood hesitant. She didn't know what to do next and began to play with her beads. I gave her a small scotch to occupy her hands and then tasted my own as I faced Yamamoto.

"Your presence is a surprise, Inspector. What have we done to arouse the interest of the Kyoto Police?"

"I am from the Osaka Police," he corrected me carefully. "To be precise I am an Inspector in the Osaka Gang Busting Squad. You must know that we have many gangsters in Japan."

"I have heard, and if you say so it must be true."

"It is true, and it is a big problem. That is why we have been obliged to set up a special force for its solution."

"I wish you every success," I said sympathetically. "But in what way does any of this concern me?"

"It concerns you because you have been observed consorting with a known gangster criminal."

"Consorting?" I repeated blankly, as though I did not understand the word.

Yamamoto nodded. "The man in question is known as Shino. We cannot afford to watch all of our criminals all the time, but occasionally we keep some of the most notorious under observation. Usually it is a waste of time. Sometimes it is not. Today, Mister Chan, you were seen in conversation with Shino and a young Japanese girl in the gardens of the golden pavilion. Then you walked away with them. My man, who was following Shino tried to keep you in sight, discreetly of course. The path you followed divided into two, and

50

unfortunately my man took the wrong fork and lost you."

"That is indeed unfortunate," I agreed. "If your man had been closer, or had maintained his surveillance for any useful length of time, then he would have realized that I was not a willing companion of these persons you have mentioned. The girl had a gun in the sleeve of her *kimono*. I was kidnapped."

Sharon looked startled, she dropped her beads and her fingers flew to her mouth. Yamamoto blinked once, very slowly. I forestalled his first question with one of my own.

"How did you learn my name, Inspector? And how did you know where to find me?"

"Miss Vale supplied that information," Yamamoto answered. "She came to us."

"I'm sorry, David," Sharon said awkwardly. "I waited in the gardens until it was almost dark. I couldn't imagine what could have happened to you, and eventually I asked a policeman if I was in the right garden. Then I asked him if he had seen you, and I had to give him a description."

"The descriptions matched," Yamamoto concluded. He gazed at me steadily through his spectacles. "You stated that you were kidnapped, Mister Chan. For what purpose?"

"As yet I don't know." For once I could be honest and evasive at the same time.

He frowned. "Please tell me exactly what happened?"

By now I had weighed all my alternatives and decided that at this stage there was nothing to be gained by holding anything back. I gave him a full account and he listened with rigid interest. When I mentioned Mister Morita his eyebrows went up again and he gave another slow blink.

"Morita," he repeated softly, as though a long coveted prize had suddenly come within his reach.

"He wore the robes of a Buddhist Grand Monk."

Yamamoto nodded. "He is a Buddhist Grand Monk — at a temple in Osaka. Here he was not at his own temple."

"What else is he?" I asked. "Who are Shino and his friends?"

Yamamoto studied me for a moment. "They are the gangster criminals I have mentioned," he said at last. "They are *Yakusa*! Have you heard of the *Yakusa*?"

"The name is familiar. Are they some sort of secret society?"

"They are a criminal organization, Mister Chan — but they are also something more. The *Yakusa* deal in crime and extortion, but they have their own rules and their own code of honour. Some of them are very powerful businessmen, and some of them operate on the lowest level in the slum areas. One of the more respectable activities of your friend Shino is that of a labour organizer in the Kamagasaki suburb of Osaka. He and his friends recruit day-to-day labour for the docks, at a percentage of course. The *Yakusa* are involved in many rackets, and membership involves an elaborate initiation ceremony. They are loyal to their organization, they protect their friends, and any of them would give their lives or their liberty for the Grand Monk. He is their spiritual head."

"It sounds like the *Mafia*," Sharon ventured.

Yamamoto nodded. "It is a good likeness, except that the American *Mafia* is based upon certain sicilian families, while the *Yakusa* regard them-selves as the descendants of honourable bandits, the wandering *samurai*."

"It all makes Mister Morita sound like a Japanese version of the Godfather," I observed wryly.

"I have seen the film." Yamamoto smiled as thought that should make us friends. Then he became serious again. "But what did they want from you, Mister Chan?"

"They seemed to think I could help them find a man named Tony Fallon."

"Who is this man?"

"An American." I looked to Sharon and allowed her to fill in the rest while I finished my drink.

"Tony is my fiancé," she explained. "We were to be married, but three weeks ago he came to Japan on a business trip and vanished. David runs a private detective agency in Hong Kong. He is helping me to search for Tony."

Yamamoto looked doubtful. Why should you engage a Hong Kong detective to find a man who is missing in Japan?"

"Because the Chan Agency was highly recommended. It's the only agency in the far east that is widely known in the United States. I don't speak any Japanese and I wouldn't know where to find a Japanese detective who spoke English."

"Many of them do," Yamamoto

remarked gently.

"But David has a brilliant reputation."

Yamamoto looked at me doubtfully. I pretended a suitable air of modesty. Yamamoto turned back to Sharon.

"What was your fiancé's business, Miss Vale."

"He was employed by Morrison and Brooks in Detroit. They import Japanese and foreign automobiles. Tony was their chief buyer."

"But in America they make so many cars, especially in Detroit."

"In America the production lines are mostly geared to the manufacture of big cars," I explained. "But due to the rising cost of oil and traffic congestion in the cities there is now an increasing demand for smaller cars. Many American families have a second car which the wife uses for shopping. Koga are trying to exploit this market with their new 1000 model which is designed to have feminine appeal. It comes in pastel colours like salmon pink, apricot and lavender."

"You seem to know a lot about Japanese cars?"

"Only because I visited the Koga car company earlier this afternoon. Tony Fallon placed an order for twenty of the new Kogas shortly before he vanished."

Yamamoto showed interest. "You have had some success in tracing this man's movements?"

I nodded and told him all that I had learned so far. He made notes while I talked and then promised to visit the *Yushimaso Ryokan* to make his own enquiries. Finally he closed his book and returned to the subject that interested him most.

"How did you escape from the *Yakusa*, Mister Chan? After your interview with Mister Morita I can hardly imagine that you were simply released."

I told him how Shino and his friends had thrown me into the path of the bullet express. Sharon looked horrified and even the inspector had to blink twice.

"Perhaps you should examine some of your suicides more carefully," I finished on a note of censure. "It might be of interest to know how many more of them were *Yakusa* murders."

"This is indeed a revelation." Yamamoto looked surprised and delighted. "Mister Chan, are you prepared to make your statement in writing and sign it? And are you prepared to testify against Shino and his colleagues in court?"

"It would be an honour and a pleasure," I assured him.

His moon face beamed happily. "Then I will send one of my men to take your statement. Meanwhile I shall leave now to order the arrest of Shino. It is a joy that I have contemplated for a long time."

"And the Grand Monk?"

His smile faded for a moment and he shrugged his shoulders.

"Mister Chan, some things are not possible. You have said that Mister Morita was not actually present when

58

you were kidnapped, and also he was not present when you were knocked down in the path of the train. It is not an offence to exchange words with you, and he can claim that he knew nothing of the manner in which you were brought before him, and nothing of the events which occurred after you left the temple. In any case Shino will accept full responsibility for everything of a criminal nature. If it is necessary he will consider it a privilege to go to prison to protect Mister Morita. It is the *Yakusa* code of honour."

"Then we must be satisfied with Shino."

"That is satisfaction enough. A good day's work, Mister Chan."

His beam had returned and he said his goodbyes and departed. He was in a hurry and forgot to close the door behind him. I closed it myself and then turned to my client.

"Now, Sharon," I said sternly. "Isn't it time you told me the truth about your fiancé?"

4

SHARON stared at me as though I had made indecent advances. Then her eyes seemed to expand into huge, candid blue lakes of bewilderment. She had finished her whisky and her right hand clenched her beads into a knot at her throat.

"David, I don't understand. I've already told you everything there is to know about Tony."

"Not everything," I contradicted. "You haven't told me what there is about Tony that is of such vital interest to the Japanese *Mafia*! They are equally as anxious to find your missing fiancé as you are, and you can be sure that they're not devoting their time and interest out of pure goodness of heart. I've already learned enough to know that the *Yakusa* is not exactly the local Salvation Army!"

"But I don't know what their interest could be. It doesn't make sense."

I tried to be patient. "Sharon, today I almost got killed, not because I was out of my depth, but because I was in deep and dangerous waters without even knowing it. I played a virtually passive hand because I didn't know the stakes in the game. I let them take me for a ride, because until the last moment I didn't realize that it was meant to be my last ride. Today I was lucky, but in this business you can't expect to live on luck alone. You led me into this blind, but before I take another step you've got to open my eyes."

"David, I'm sorry. I didn't know that anything like this was going to happen. It's all come as a complete shock."

Her voice was wretched but she still wasn't offering any answers. I decided that it was going to be a long job and mixed us both another drink before I steered her into a chair. Then I sat down to face her.

"Alright, Sharon, you didn't know and I didn't know — but now we both know that searching for Tony is not going to be safe or easy. And I think we both know that you haven't been totally honest with me. Now is the time to make a fresh start. If that's impossible then I'm taking the next plane back to Hong Kong."

"But, David, you can't. I have to find Tony!"

"Then you have to stop holding back information."

"But you know he was here in Kyoto. You know where he stayed. It shouldn't be difficult to find out what happened to him from there. You have a reputation — "

"Not for getting myself killed," I cut in bluntly. "And not for getting my clients killed either. I tried to cover you today by pretending that you were only my secretary, but you could still be at risk. If you stay on alone to look for Tony then you could become the next kidnap victim of the *Yakusa*."

That scared her. She took a long nervous pull at her whisky and then decided to open up; "Alright, David, there were some little things I didn't tell you. But I didn't think they were important." She looked at me earnestly. "They're not even definite things — just my own doubts. Things I didn't think you would need to know."

"Let's start right from the beginning," I suggested. "You told me that Tony came to Japan on a routine business trip. Was that the truth?"

She wriggled with embarrassment. She crossed her legs which were long and shapely, but whether that was an effort to distract me or not she quickly changed her mind and uncrossed them again. She smoothed the hem of her skirt towards her knees with one hand, and then finally she decided to look at me.

"It wasn't quite the truth," she admitted. "Tony left Detroit without giving me any reason. In fact he didn't even tell me that he was leaving."

She stopped and I had to prompt her to go on.

"I called round at Tony's apartment and found it empty. I had a key that he gave me when we were engaged." She showed me the blue sapphire ring on her finger as proof of the engagement. It was expensive and matched the colour of her eyes.

"The wardrobe was open and I saw that his suitcase had gone and all his clothes. Then I found his bank book in the wastepaper basket. It was cancelled. He had drawn out all his money, a little over ten thousand dollars, and closed the account. I just couldn't understand it. We were due to be married and he hadn't given any sign that he was walking out."

"How did you know that he came to Japan?"

"There was a JAL Airlines flight schedule in the wastepaper basket. A flight number was ringed in ink so I called the airline office and checked. They confirmed that Tony had booked on that flight to Tokyo."

"And was he on his firm's business?"

"No." She moved uncomfortably in her chair. "I called Morrison and Brooks, but they knew nothing about Tony's trip."

"So why did you tell me that Tony was on a routine business trip?"

"It was only a white lie, David. I couldn't bring myself to tell you — or anyone — that Tony had simply quit Detroit without even saying goodbye. I figured you might think that Tony had decided not to marry me and taken the easy way out. Then you wouldn't have bothered to look for him."

"Did he take the easy way out?"

"No." She finished her scotch in one gulp and put the empty glass down. Her hand went back to her beads. "Tony wouldn't run out on me. I'm sure of that. He *wanted* to marry me."

"So why didn't he kiss you goodbye? Why did he come to Japan?"

"I don't know."

"But you must have thought about it. You must have turned over a few possibilities in your mind."

"I've done nothing else. All I can think of is that he must be in some kind of trouble. He must need help."

"What sort of trouble?"

"I don't know, David. I just don't know."

"Trouble with the law?" I suggested bluntly.

"Maybe. Yes — " She looked confused. "I suppose that is what I thought. But I don't want to jump to the wrong conclusion. I don't want you to jump to the wrong conclusion. I just want to find him and talk to him. I want to give him a chance to explain before I make any judgements."

"What crime was Tony in a position to commit?"

"None that I know of."

"Could he have fiddled an account or a computer and absconded with a few million dollars belonging to Morrison and Brooks?"

66

"No. If he had then they would have known that something was wrong when I called. Besides, Tony isn't a thief. He wouldn't do anything like that."

"Did he have a criminal record of any kind?"

"No." She began to look frustrated and angry. "He was just a nice, ordinary guy. He had a good job, some money in the bank, and we were in love. We had the wedding all planned."

"How long had you known him?"

"About a year."

"Not long."

"Long enough," she insisted defensively.

We became silent. For the moment I had run out of questions. I had got a few answers but so far I had not learned much more. Tony Fallon had not vanished in Japan on a normal business trip. Instead he had walked out on her in Detroit and then vanished in Japan on some mysterious errand of his own. If that was progress it was hardly a great step forward. It didn't tell me where he was now, or why he was wanted by the *Yakusa.*

"David." Sharon was looking worried. She leaned forward and her hand touched my knee. "You will stay and help me to find Tony?"

Her eyes were appealing, but I remembered Belinda's warning. The story Sharon had just told me had sounded very convincing, but I remembered that she had sounded equally truthful when we had first met in the agency office. She had only told part of her story then, so I felt justified in wondering whether there was still more to come, or whether the whole thing might be a complete fiction.

To stall I asked her to tell me again how she had come to select the Chan Agency as the most logical recipient for her troubles.

She looked affronted. "David, I've told you before — you were recommended."

"By whom?"

"A private investigator in Detroit. I went to him initially for help. He said that as Tony had gone to Japan I needed someone who operated in the far east. He'd heard of the Chan Agency through your American partner, Tracey Ryan."

"Tracey is a New Yorker. She's never been to Detroit."

"Well maybe he knew her in New York. I don't know that he always operated in Detroit. I don't even know that he actually knew her in a personal sense. Maybe he just heard of her."

"What was his name?"

She hesitated. "Miller — Hank Miller."

I made a mental note and became thoughtful. Sharon watched me and it was obvious she was still worried that I might quit.

"What will you do next?" she asked nervously.

I didn't hurry to answer. Finding Tony Fallon wasn't going to be the straightforward job it had first seemed, and there were aspects of the case that I definitely didn't like. At the same time it was always difficult to pull out of a case once the investigation had started. It was bad professionally and my ego didn't like it. I was a Chinese Bulldog and once I got my teeth into something then I hated to let go. Also I had a score to settle with Shino and his fat friends. The last thought made me realize that it was doubtful whether Yamamoto would let me leave Japan anyway. He wanted his statement and my testimony to nail Shino and strike a blow at the *Yakusa*. My return to Hong Kong would be delayed, so I might as well finish the job.

"There are only three people who knew that I was looking for Tony," I said at last. "One was Ken Kenichi, the Tokyo detective who did the initial spadework and traced Tony here to Kyoto. Two was Mister Sato, the manager of the *Yushimaso Ryokan* where Tony stayed. And three was

Mister Shinjira, the Chairman of the Koga car company. One of them called in the *Yakusa* — and I know which one told me a pack of lies. That's where I'll start again tomorrow."

★ ★ ★

I intended an early start but I was delayed until almost noon by two polite young police officers from Inspector Yamamoto's Gang Busting Squad. They arrived with a portable typewriter, took down my detailed statement, and smiled happily when I signed it. Their smiles faded when I asked if Shino had actually been arrested as promised, and they shook their heads regretfully. "Not yet," the senior man said, "But soon." I hoped that their optimism was justified.

When they departed I followed after ten minutes on the road to Osaka. I was driving a red Datsun saloon that I had hired for the duration of my stay in Japan. Sharon had elected to stay behind at the hotel. Yesterday she had explored Kyoto's heritage of temples and shrines while I worked, but after hearing of my experiences she had become wary of those beautifully landscaped gardens.

Osaka was twenty-seven miles southwest of Kyoto, less than forty minutes drive on the fast expressway. It was also a journey from one world to another. Much of Kyoto was Old Japan, the ancient capital steeped in historical association and rich with mythology and legend. While most of Osaka was New Japan, a giant commercial and industrial centre with a swollen population, situated on the mouth of the Yodo River. Its heart was an area of huge modern banks, office blocks and department stores, with magnificent flyover roads spanning the river and canals. Its body was a vast, bloated, grey-hazed blur of sprawling docks and factories.

The Koga car factory was a giant complex on the south side of the city.

The front building that housed the administration and sales offices was a clinical palace of polished glass and white concrete. It was a six storey building over a hundred yards wide with an eight story central tower flying the company flag. The name Koga was written in splendid blood red letters above each wing. To reach this edifice of industrial imperialism it was necessary to drive between ranks of hundreds upon hundreds of finished cars, all parked on either side of the approach road. They were all the new Koga 1000 model, ice green, turquoise blue and cherry red, with a scattering of the softer, pastel colours destined for the American housewife market. It was a colourful and impressive sight.

I noticed that the building was still draped with the red star flags of Communist China. Two weeks previously a Chinese trade delegation had toured the factory and the flags had been raised in their honour. Perhaps they were expected to return, for I remembered vaguely that the trade delegation was still in Japan. It had moved on to Nagoya.

I parked my car and went into the main entrance hall. Electronically controlled glass doors slid back smoothly as I approached and a girl in a white *kimono* bowed as I entered. It was like stepping into a plush hotel. I stated my business and was politely requested to wait for just one moment. Many moments and a succession of receptionists went by before I eventually reached the sixth floor where Mister Shinjira had his audience hall and throne of power.

His secretary was the last barrier, a petite little Japanese girl who wore a dark skirt, a snow white jumper and a delightfully sunny smile. Her black hair had been cut in a neat fringe over intelligent brown eyes, and at the back of her neck it was tied in a long, glossy ponytail.

"Mister Chan," she greeted me warmly. "I did not expect you to return.

Today Mister Shinjira is extremely busy."

"I am sure that Mister Shinjira is always extremely busy," I returned politely. "But it is important that I see him."

"But you saw him yesterday. I understand that your business was concluded. Today you do not have an appointment. And Mister Shinjira's time is very valuable."

I borrowed a pen from her desk and a sheet of paper. I wrote down one word, folded the paper and handed it to her.

"Please, take this to Mister Shinjira. I feel sure that he will spare me a few more moments of his time."

She looked puzzled but then nodded. I waited for her to return and when she did reappear she held open the door to the inner sanctum. Her expression was still creased with a faintly bewildered frown.

"Mister Shinjira will see you now."

I smiled at her and then walked into

the chairman's office.

Mister Shinjira stood beside his desk. He was a man full of quick, restless energy who found difficulty in sitting still. He had a high, flat forehead, deeply lined with wrinkles although he was only in his fifties. His long face looked sour and now there was an angry twist to his mouth. Yesterday he had granted me an interview cordially enough, but now he did not bow or smile. He shoved my improvised calling card back at me and demanded:

"Mister Chan, what does this mean?"

The sheet of paper was badly crumpled. The girl secretary had carried it very carefully so I had to assume that it had been crushed in Shinjira's fist. The word *Yakusa*, printed in block capitals, was still just legible.

"It means that after I left here yesterday these people followed me, kidnapped me, and tried to kill me." I spoke softly, watching his face. His jaw was tense and a muscle twitched high in his cheek. "They were interested

76

in Tony Fallon," I continued. "They followed me from Osaka back to Kyoto, and the only person in Osaka who knew that I was making enquiries about Tony Fallon was you, Mister Shinjira!"

5

SHINJIRA looked astonished, both at the bluntness of my insinuation and at its meaning. His jaw dropped, revealing silver-capped teeth and he stared at me in horror. The wrinkles deepened in his flat forehead. Either he was genuinely shocked or he was putting on a very good act.

I thought back over the polite atmosphere in which our first interview had been conducted, and over all that I knew about Japanese industrialists in general. A company chairman in Japan was an economic emperor, commanding a devotion and obedience from his subjects second only to that inspired by the ancient Son of Heaven in his imperial palace in Tokyo. A firm the size of Koga cars was *Zaibatsu*, an interlocked conglomeration of financial and business interests that was a world of its own and a power equal to any in the land. It was its own welfare state, controlling the life, death and burial of all its millions of dependants. Shinjira was Uncle, God and Dictator. A man in his position would be unaccustomed to acting.

On the other hand I knew that he had worked his way up through the junior executive ranks. On the way he would have fawned, bowed and smiled with the same self-effacing discipline of the ambitious young men who were beneath him now. The essential display of servile loyalty that Japanese business ethics demanded of its juniors was in itself an act in a man determined upon reaching the topmost pinnacle of the chairman's office. I wondered if Mister Shinjira could ever reign here long enough to forget how to give a convincing performance.

"Mister Chan," he said sharply. "Please explain what you imply."

The direct approach had not been conclusive so now I smiled an apology and returned to tact.

"I fear that someone in your employ must have notified these people of my visit yesterday afternoon." I spoke carefully and went on to give him a full account of what had happened. He listened impassively but his eyes flickered twice, when I named the Grand Monk Morita and when I mentioned my narrow escape from the bullet express.

"Mister Chan, this is monstrous," he said at last. "To think that you who were my guest should be subjected to such an encounter within an hour of leaving this office is unbelievable!" His expression was one of righteous anger which changed over a slow pause to one of frowning indignation. Then he continued with equal firmness: "But to believe that anyone at Koga cars could be in any way involved is also unthinkable. Every single employee of this company is unquestionably loyal. I know that in any other country of the world this would be nonsense, but in Japan it is the truth."

I nodded politely. "The Japanese bond that exists between all levels of industry is a marvel that is envied in the west. But even so the events of yesterday require an explanation. How could the *Yakusa* know, within minutes after I had left this office, that you and I had been discussing the disappearance of Tony Fallon?"

Shinjira spread his hands helplessly. "There is no answer."

"There is the telephone." I pointed to the white telephone on his desk. "Not necessarily this telephone, there must be many in a building of this size. The question is not really one of which telephone, but one of who made the call?"

He looked more hurt now than angry. "Mister Chan, I have assured you that I have complete trust in every person who works for Koga cars, and especially in everyone who has access to this floor level. My fellow executives, my junior aides, and even my secretaries are all

81

above suspicion. They are devoted to myself and the company. Do you know, Mister Chan — " His chest puffed and his voice rang with pride. "If I so much as leave this office for one day, just to fly to Tokyo for a business lunch, then my entire staff will follow me to the airport to bid me farewell. They will wish me luck, they will wish me a safe return, they will sing the company anthem — and there will be tears in their eyes. That is the measure of their devotion!"

I knew that he did not exaggerate, for I had witnessed such a scene at Tokyo's Haneda Airport on my arrival.

I was silent. Shinjira stared at me for a moment and then he waved me to a chair. He went behind his desk and sat down. He was thoughtful for a moment and then he spoke again.

"Nevertheless, you have made a serious accusation, and it must be investigated. I will personally question all my staff. It will be painful, but I shall do it. If I have been betrayed then I shall discover the culprit. And you will be informed, Mister Chan. I promise you."

"Thank you, Mister Shinjira." There was not much else I could say to such a speech. He waited for me to take my leave, but there was another point I had to raise.

"There is one more thing," I said slowly. "Yesterday you told me that Tony Fallon visited you to place an order for Koga cars on behalf of Morrison and Brooks in Detroit. Last night I learned that Fallon was no longer employed by Morrison and Brooks." I made a delicate pause. "I must confess that I find myself confused."

Again he stared at me. His eyes were uncertain but then he half smiled. "You are not confused, Mister Chan. You see clearly another mystery."

He stood up again and walked over to the window where I could not see his face. He gazed out for thirty seconds and then swung back to look at me.

"Very well, I admit that yesterday I misled you. I apologize. Mister Fallon did not come here to place an order. He came to sell me an artist's design for a new style of car — which I declined."

"Why?"

"For two reasons. One is that I have Japanese artists in my design offices here who are producing much better work. The other is that I knew Mister Fallon was not an artist, and not a designer. I suspected his drawings may have been stolen."

"I understand." I smiled at him blandly. "But why was it necessary to mislead me?"

"I feared scandal, Mister Chan. Not for myself," he added piously. "But for the Koga car company. Our reputation is of the highest. Our honesty is beyond refute. I did not want it known that a thief would even consider bringing a stolen design to Koga cars. I pray that this is something you can truly understand?"

Again I assured him that I fully understood.

★ ★ ★

I left the Koga car building reflecting that a man who would lie once could lie twice, or even three times. I still had deep doubts about Mister Shinjira. I reached my parked car and stopped to unlock the door and it was then I realized that I had been followed. The chairman's last-barrier secretary, the little Japanese girl with the sunny smile, was standing at my elbow. She had hurried, for her coat was still unfastened, and her smooth face was both embarrassed and anxious.

"Mister Chan, if you are returning to Osaka city, may I accompany you, please?"

"It will be my pleasure," I told her politely.

I got into the car and opened the passenger door for her. She slipped in quickly beside me and glanced up once at the overlooking ranks of windows. We were not in immediate view of the chairman's window but she was obviously nervous. I drove away promptly to allay her fears.

She was silent until we were on the main road. Then she gave me a shy, sideways glance. Some of her anxiety had gone but her embarrassment was still there.

"Thank you for giving me a ride, Mister Chan. It was only a few minutes to my lunch time and today is my afternoon off. Usually half of it is wasted while I wait for the buses."

"Call me David," I said to put her at ease.

She smiled. "My name is Naoka."

We chatted pleasantly for a few more minutes, but she had something on her mind and eventually it emerged.

"I saw what you had written on the piece of paper you sent in to Mister Shinjira," she said awkwardly. "And — and I overheard some of your conversation over the office intercom."

She blushed and looked down at her hands in her lap.

I slowed the car so that I could look at her without risking an accident. Most Japanese drove like *kamikaze* pilots and the traffic on the expressway was somewhat hectic.

"Is that why you followed me?"

She nodded and then met my eyes. Her face was serious.

"David, the *Yakusa* does have connections within the Koga factory. They are everywhere. They virtually control the trade union. It is the *Yakusa* men who push the negotiations for better pay and conditions. Much of the organization of labour movement in Japan is the work of the *Yakusa*."

"Are they represented on the managerial level?"

"It is possible. I do not know."

"Could Mister Shinjira be a member of the *Yakusa*?"

"Again it is possible, many very powerful people are *Yakusa*. But again I do not know."

I found a safe place to pull off the road and stop the car. I switched off the ignition and then twisted in my seat to face her directly. She looked very innocent and very vulnerable. They were both qualities which I was beginning to distrust.

"Naoka," I said softly. "Why are you telling me all this?"

She blushed, her cheeks becoming almost as pink as the cherry blossom in a nearby garden.

"I want to help," she said in a low voice. "Tony was a very good friend to me. If he is in trouble I want to help him."

"What sort of a friend?"

"We went out together, every time he was in Osaka. Sometimes to a nightclub or a restaurant. Sometimes to *Kabuki* theatre or the ballet. He bought me many presents. We were very close."

"Did you go out together on his last visit to Osaka?"

"No." Her face became sad. "We

arranged to go out when Tony came to visit Mister Shinjira. Tony promised to collect me from my apartment the same evening, but he never came."

"Have you heard from him since then?"

She shook her head. "I have expected him to telephone, or to call at my apartment, but there has been nothing. At first I was angry, then I became puzzled. Now I am very worried. I think that something bad must have happened to Tony."

I glanced at my watch and saw that it was past noon.

"Let me buy you lunch today," I suggested. "Then you can tell me everything you know about Tony Fallon."

★ ★ ★

We dined in a seafood restaurant in the centre of the city where every dish was excellent except for the slices of raw fish. Afterwards the sun was shining and we paid a visit to Osaka Castle, a magnificent white *donjon* with elaborate green, sloping roofs. It rose like a tiered oriental pyramid from a base constructed with massive, grey-stone blocks. After we had passed through the monumental outer walls and over the bridge spanning the wide moat we entered the park and flower gardens that surrounded the castle. Here we were able to stroll quietly and talk.

This was where it had begun, Naoka confided. A year ago on one of his earlier visits to Japan, Tony Fallon had paused to say hello after a meeting with Shinjira at Koga cars. He had suggested that she might like to show him the sights of Osaka on her afternoon off and she had allowed herself to be persuaded. They had visited the castle, and then all the various temples and shrines in the city. On his later visits they had made trips to Kyoto and Nara, and once a two-day cruise on the Inland Sea.

The picture that emerged during the course of the afternoon was of a cheerful, free-spending young American who had found a pretty Japanese girl to share his free time whenever his business brought him to Japan. Their hours together had been fun. Tony was Number One, Naoka said, and her blushes conveyed that they had been lovers.

By the end of the afternoon we were firm friends and I drove her home to her apartment in the southern suburbs. It was a grey block in an area of grey blocks, and I suspected that this one was subsidised or owned by Koga cars. She lived in two rooms on the third floor, a tiny, brightly-gleaming kitchen, and a second small room that was divided even further by sliding screens. There was no furniture in the western sense, just bright silk cushions on the *tatami*, two low level tables, one supporting a vase of large yellow chrysanthemums, a compact television with a ten-inch screen, and equally compact stereo equipment. There were two scrolls on the walls, prayers composed of Japanese characters brush-drawn on white rice paper.

"Will you have coffee, David?" She repeated the invitation that had brought me up here. Then she added as an afterthought: "Or perhaps you would prefer tea? Have you ever witnessed the Japanese tea ceremony?"

I had to admit that I had not.

She smiled at me, amused by her own thoughts.

"It is an honour," she said. "I will show you."

She put a record on the stereo and bade me wait while she disappeared behind the screen. I spent five minutes listening to Duke Ellington, and thinking about Tony Fallon, before she called for me to join her.

She was kneeling on the *tatami* in a beautiful bronze-coloured *kimono*, with a deep red sash secured by a white cord. Before her was a silver urn on a small gas fire, the cups and bowl and other essentials for the tea ceremony. She smiled up at me.

"You must kneel, David. You will find it all terribly boring and your legs will ache, but you must pretend that you are enjoying every moment and pay me many pretty compliments. Otherwise you will be very bad-mannered."

She was laughing at me which meant that she was not really serious. I knelt and she handed me a white napkin and a small plum cake with a sliver of birch wood to use as a fork.

"You must tell me it is delicious, even if it is awful."

I ate the cake carefully. "It is delicious," I agreed.

She smiled and began to prepare the tea. There was a whole ritual of washing and carefully drying the already spotless utensils, and it seemed that every item had to be revolved three times on every occasion that it was touched. Measuring out and making the tea was an equally slow and religious task and my knees were soon sore where they pressed on the hard straw matting. Naoka laughed some more and chided me when I flexed a muscle in a cramped leg, and insisted that I must praise the shape and design of her cups.

When the tea was ready it looked like a thin green soup. She revolved the cup three times before placing it on the mat beside my right knee. She bowed to me deeply and recited some words in Japanese.

"Now you must bow to me," she instructed. "Then you must turn the cup three times. Then you must taste the tea slowly. Then you must tell me it is the most wonderful tea that has ever passed your lips."

I wondered briefly if the tea was drugged, but then decided that it was unlikely. Yesterday I had been unsuspecting and today I was probably over suspicious. Slowly I performed the ritual as she had described.

"It is the most wonderful tea I have ever tasted," I assured her.

She laughed aloud. "David, it is horrible — I know. Next you will ask me what it all means."

"What does it all mean?"

"I don't know," she shrugged helplessly. "Some say that it is a tradition invented by the priests to make us patient and polite with each other. Others say it was invented by the *Shoguns* to give the Japanese less time to involve themselves with plots of assassination."

It was all a meaningless joke and she was still smiling as she helped me up and steered me back into the main part of the room. I killed time patiently as I listened to her moving behind the screen. I guessed that she was clearing her props away and changing out of the luxurious *kimono*. I puzzled over why she had wasted our time, and then she called out to me again, more softly and seductively than before.

I moved behind the screen and found

that she had unrolled a mattress on the floor. On the mattress, beneath a single white silk sheet, lay Naoka. Her shoulders were bare, and the sheet was moulded to the contours of her small breasts and between her thighs with a closeness that showed she was naked. Her sunny smile was beaming up at me.

"Is this still a part of the tea ceremony?" I asked politely.

"Only for very honoured guests," she answered, and stretched out her arms towards me.

★ ★ ★

There are times when my job pays delightful dividends, and this was one of those times. Naoka had a warm enthusiasm for sex that built up quickly into a hot and passionate exuberance. Desire burned within her with hungry flames. Her fingers, lips and tongue explored eagerly while her body squirmed with anticipation. The fact that it was totally unexpected made it doubly exciting. After seeing her robed like an imperial princess in the rich dignity of the *kimono* it was an added thrill to feel her naked flesh in my arms. While the gentle restraint of the tea ceremony now seemed to emphasise her abandoned sexuality. It was like finding a queen with the hidden dash of a nymphomaniac adventuress; a virgin with the skills of a geisha.

I sensed that Naoka received her own kicks from the transformation, and when we reached the heights we found that we had scaled a volcano where the whole universe was an ecstatic explosion of molten lava. It was carnal Krakatoa!

★ ★ ★

We lay spent and for a while we were silent. Then she stirred in my arms and began to murmur sweet pillow talk, praising my virility, and prompting return compliments on her own feminine virtues. Time passed pleasantly and then she revealed the eternal woman's curiosity.

"Is Japanese girl as good as American girl?"

"Japanese girl is Number One," I told her diplomatically. "Very, very superior."

She smiled happily. "Is Naoka better than the American girl who is with you at Kyoto?"

"Naoka is better than any girl I have ever known. She is the sweetest woman I have ever tasted."

She snuggled closer to my chest, content and flattered, but she was single-minded.

"Tell me about this American girl who says that she is going to marry my Tony."

I detected a subtle change in our relationship. All through the afternoon I had asked the questions, although I had been obliged to mention Sharon Vale to explain my own interest in Tony Fallon. Now the positions were reversed and it was Naoka who was probing for answers. I gave them to her but made sure they contained as little practical information as possible. She became frustrated and the naive cover questions that were designed to make me believe she was merely jealous of her American lover's fiancé became fewer.

Finally I yawned gently. "I am becoming thirsty," I informed her blandly.

"I have some *saki*. I will fetch it."

She kissed me and then slipped quickly out of bed. Her white bottom bobbed through the screens as she hurried away.

I moved swiftly. There was one cupboard built into the wall with a sliding door, but inside there was only her *kimono*, her day clothes and the tea utensils. I looked through the screens into the main part of the room and saw that Naoka was hidden in the kitchen. The door was half closed behind her.

There were only a limited number

of possible hiding places and so it took only a matter of seconds to find what I was certain would be there. The tape recorder was under one of the silken cushions that leaned against the dividing screen. It was a miniature recorder and the two inch diameter tapes were revolving slowly and silently.

Despite the fact that this was Japan, the oriental fountainhead for sophisticated electronics, I noticed immediately that the tape recorder had been manufactured in Red China.

6

IT was late in the evening when I returned to Kyoto and Sharon was waiting for me. I had telephoned the hotel earlier in the afternoon to warn her that I would be unavoidably delayed, so she was only just beginning to worry. I poured us both a scotch, a vast improvement on the watered-gin taste of *saki*, and when we were comfortable I recited a suitably censored account of my day's adventures. She was employing me and paying my expenses so I owed her that much.

The fact that her intended husband had enjoyed an amorous dalliance with a pretty Japanese girl did not upset her as I expected. Instead she remained surprisingly calm.

"Are you sure that this girl knew Tony?"

"Reasonably sure, she seemed to

know a great deal about him. She claims she had a date with him on the night he left the *ryokan* and vanished. He should have collected her at her apartment at eight o'clock but he didn't show up. She called the hotel where he normally stayed in Osaka, but of course he wasn't there. Apparently she didn't know that on this occasion he was staying in Kyoto."

I paused. "Why do you think Tony chose to stay in Kyoto when his business contacts and his girl friend were all in Osaka?"

"I have no idea." Sharon looked blank.

"It does suggest that he wanted to avoid his usual haunts where he could easily be located." I frowned and then asked: "What do you think of Shinjira's new story, that Tony tried to sell him a set of possibly stolen design drawings for a new car?"

"I don't believe it," she said loyally. But her face registered her doubts. She was beginning to realize by now that the truth, when it was finally known, would not prove to be wholly pleasant.

"I don't believe it either," I consoled her. "Shinjira had to change his story when he learned that Tony was no longer working for his old firm, but if his second story was true then there was no logical reason why he should not have told me the first time we met. His fear of involving the company in a scandal doesn't hold water. There must be another reason why Tony visited Koga cars, but I'm convinced that we won't hear it from Shinjira."

"What about this secretary — Naoka?"

"Perhaps." I had left Naoka without revealing that I had discovered her Chinese tape recorder, so our pseudo-friendship was still intact. "But first there's another line of enquiry that I want to follow. Tomorrow I intend to take a trip to Tokyo."

★ ★ ★

I left the hotel before dawn the next morning and drove for an hour before the sun rose. It could have been a pleasant excursion, passing rice fields and small towns, gardens filled with cherry and plum blossom, green hills and distant mountains, and the cities of Nagoya, Toyohashi, Shizuoka and Yokohama. However, Sharon did not accompany me and I was in a hurry. The shrines, castles and *tori* gateways that we might have stopped to investigate went by in a blur.

By noon I had found a new respect for the robust little Datsun, and weary and with aching back muscles I arrived on the great flyover expressway above the heart of greater Tokyo. I drove down into Chuo-dori Avenue and an office block that was only a stone's throw away from the glittering department stores of the Ginza.

Ken Kenichi had his private investigator's office on the seventh floor.

His secretary remembered me and bowed me smoothly into his presence.

He was engaged in the eternal occupation of the private eye, pretending to be so busily in demand that he could not possibly be interested in another case, except as a personal favour or at an extortionate price. However, when he saw me he relaxed and turned away from his files. He was a middle-aged Japanese in a western suit, neat and lean with bright eyes and a wide smile. His teeth flashed at me now.

"David Chan, my honoured friend, you are again welcome."

"I need some more help," I admitted as we shook hands. "Some information."

"Please tell me." He waved me to a chair and in virtually the same movement produced a bottle of Japanese whisky and two glasses from beneath his desk. "I remember that you are not fond of *saki*." He poured two healthy shots and then asked, "Have you succeeded in finding your mysterious Mister Fallon?"

"Not yet," I said wryly, and proceeded to tell him about my search to date. He listened with his head cocked slightly on one side, not touching his whisky. I knew that when he did remember it he would down it at a gulp.

Ken Kenichi had qualified as a lawyer and practised for ten years before deciding that courtroom life was too dull and too routine. It was then that he had decided to quit his profession and take on the less certain but more varied role of a private investigator. Such individuality in a regimented society made him almost unique in Japan, but he had a talent for detective work, which combined with his law background and a seemingly endless mental storage capacity for all types of facts and information made him an immediate success.

Often a major enquiry would overlap two countries and it would be necessary for one agency to recruit the services and resources of another. In Japan I had always found Kenichi efficient and reliable, and in return he had occasionally called upon the Chan

Agency when there was a Hong Kong angle to a case of his own.

He listened attentively, inserting a question here and there like a surgeon's knife, peeling back an obscurity that I had missed. When I had finished he was thoughtful.

"It should have been a simple task," he said at last. "When I traced Fallon to Kyoto I felt that I could have closed the case myself, and that there was no real necessity for you and your client to come to Japan. But you seem to have found a number of complications. What exactly do you want from me now?"

"Some ideas might be useful. Can you think of any reason why the *Yakusa* should be interested in this affair?"

"There are many things that could interest the *Yakusa*, but there is nothing that is obvious in what you have told me."

"Some information then."

"About the *Yakusa*?"

"No, I think I got all I need there

from Inspector Yamamoto. But I would like to know everything there is to know about Shinjira and Koga cars."

"Shinjira is an important man in Japan," Kenichi said carefully. "He is one of the new, pragmatic breed of businessmen who model themselves upon the west. He is a very clever man, he has been called an industrial genius and a financial wizard even by his enemies. He is also a hard worker, he devotes all his waking hours to Koga cars. And of course he is a family man, he has a wife and two daughters. He is often photographed in their company. At the same time he will think nothing of surrounding himself with a score of expensive geisha girls at a business dinner."

Kenichi smiled. "He pilots his own helicopter and belongs to the most elite golf clubs in Osaka and Tokyo. He is highly respected in modern Japan."

"Tell me about Koga cars."

"Koga is a big company, not quite so monolithic as Toyota or Datsun, but still very big. They are a successful company, their cars are sold in Africa, Australia, America and Europe. However, Koga is a subsidiary of Osaka Oil. This is what makes Shinjira such a powerful man, he not only controls over thirty-five percent of the stocks and shares in Koga cars, he also has a seat on the board of directors and owns twenty-five percent of Osaka Oil."

I pondered over this new revelation. "It would seem to put Shinjira far above any need to consort with common gangsters."

Kenichi nodded solemn agreement, but then found ways of contradicting himself. "Remember that the *Yakusa* are not common gangsters. They organize labour and this means that sometimes industry has to deal with *Yakusa* representatives. In fact it is not unknown for industry and the *Yakusa* to combine in the exploitation of the workers."

It was all food for thought but it wasn't bringing me any immediate answers. I decided to put it all in abeyance for a while and changed the subject.

"What can you tell me about this Red Chinese trade delegation that is currently touring Japan?"

He looked surprised by the switch but his mind moved smoothly to cope, responding like the feed-out from a computer.

"The delegation numbers about thirty officials. They arrived in Japan for a three week visit which is now almost over. Officially they are here to discuss trade and exports, but they have been combining business with pleasure. They have been visiting factories and cultural shrines in approximately equal numbers. Their tour began in Osaka, from there they visited Kyoto, Nara, Nagoya and Yokahoma. Today they are visiting factories in Tokyo. Tomorrow they are scheduled to visit Nikko and the Toshogu shrine. Then I believe they return to Osaka and Kobe."

He stopped and gazed into my eyes. "Why do you ask?"

"For three reasons. One is that the trade delegation visited the Koga car factory only two days before Tony Fallon. Another is that the Japanese girl who was set to spy upon me used a tape recorder that was made in Red China. And the third is that the *Yakusa* kidnapped me because they believed I was an agent of the Red Chinese. Shino accused me point-blank of being a Chinese spy!"

"I see." The way Kenichi spoke it was almost the fatuous *Ah so!*, that was so often credited to the Japanese, but there was nothing foolish in his expression and his eyes were shrewd. He calculated my thoughts exactly.

"If you wish to get close to the Chinese then tomorrow is your only chance. You could not join them on a factory tour, or at any of the civic banquets that have been given in their honour, but there will be many ordinary visitors and tourists at the Toshogu Shrine."

"How far is Nikko from Tokyo?"

"About ninety miles to the north. Two hours by train, perhaps two and a half if you take your car." He paused. "There will be security around the Chinese, their own, and the Japanese Special Branch."

"I have no hostile intentions. Perhaps I will wave a Chairman Mao banner to reassure them."

We both smiled.

"You can sleep at my home for this afternoon," Kenichi offered. "Then you will be fresh to drive on to Nikko this evening. If there is anything else I can do you have only to ask."

I capitalized on his hospitality. "I need to make a telephone call," I said after I had expressed my gratitude. "To the Chan Agency in Hong Kong."

★ ★ ★

Twenty minutes later I was talking to Belinda Carrington.

"Hello, David," she said cheerfully. "I hope you're behaving yourself amongst all those naughty geisha girls."

"I'm a paragon of virtue," I said lightly. "How are things on the home front?"

"Tracey is still working at the clinic, she hasn't cracked the drugs-theft case yet but she feels she's getting close. I'm just opening the office mail and painting my fingernails. Are you sure you couldn't use me in Japan?"

"Our client wouldn't stand the extra expenses, but there is something you can do for me."

"And I thought you telephoned just to hear my voice."

"Belinda, I love you, but this is serious. I want you to search our files and find a reputable detective agency in Detroit. Then sub-contract part of this case. I need to know everything there is to know about Tony Fallon — and about Sharon Vale. Pass on everything she gave to us and let's see what else can be dug up."

"If you're double-checking on our client then we can hardly put it down to expenses," Belinda said dubiously. "We could end up out of pocket."

I didn't want to worry her with the fact that I could end up dead. "It's important," I insisted.

"Okay, David. I'll do it."

"One more thing. If you can find out his address you could do worse than use a man named Hank Miller. Check whether he's ever heard of Sharon Vale."

7

IT was eleven o'clock on the following morning when I drove the red Datsun over the Daiya River which flowed clear and blue over a stony bed in a green flanked gorge. Beside the main road bridge was a traditional hump-backed wooden bridge lacquered a brilliant red and reserved for ceremonial occasions. I turned left to the parking lots at the foot of the valley that led up between avenues of magnificent cedar trees and green mountain slopes to the Toshogu Shrine. I had stayed overnight at a *ryokan* in Nikko and then delayed over a late breakfast to ensure that the Chinese would arrive ahead of me. I knew that I could not afford to arouse the attention of the Japanese Special Branch by turning up too soon and killing any waiting time on the spot.

115

As I eased the Datsun into a parking space I saw that there was one large tourist coach separate from the others. There were three official-looking black cars close by but all other vehicles were being steered well clear by the park attendants. There were an unnecessary large number of attendants and I recognized the red flag of China on the isolated coach. The trade delegation was obviously ahead of me.

I locked up the Datsun and headed up the main avenue of cedars towards the shrine. There were plenty of routine visitors as Kenichi had foreseen, so I was not out of place with my jacket over my arm and a new Yashica camera slung casually around my neck. The sun was shining and it was a glorious day. I had other things on my mind but as I walked I could not escape a deep appreciation of the natural beauty of the area. Even without the cultural heritage surrounding the revered tomb of Ieyasu, the great *Shogun* who had completed the unification of medieval

116

Japan in the early seventeenth century, the head of the valley would still have rated a visit for its scenic grandeur. The whole of the surrounding area had been designated a national park.

I climbed up the steep paths to the Rinnoji Temple, the main hall was a splendid building lacquered red and black with the traditional curved grey roofs. Inside were three huge golden images of Buddhas, the Thousand-Handed Goddess of Mercy, Amida, and the Horse-Headed Kannon, each one seated upon a golden lotus. A large throng of visitors milled in and around the temple precincts but there was no sign of the Chinese.

I continued along an avenue of the giant cedars. As diminutive saplings they had been the gift of an impoverished feudal lord who could not match the lavish offerings of his wealthy contemporaries who had gilded the shrine. Now, more than three hundred years later, the dark green glory of the tall cedars threw shadows over all. It was a gentle moral amongst the splendour.

At the head of the avenue a flight of steps led up through a *tori* of grey granite. On the left of the flat-topped archway was an elegant five storey pagoda, a hundred feet high with its spire level with the tops of the cedars. Ahead was the Niomon gateway, the main entrance to the Toshogu Shrine, guarded by the fearsome images of two Deva Kings.

I found the Red Chinese trade delegation just beyond the gateway, gazing up in awe at the sculpted eaves and carved and colourful decorations of the sacred storehouses and stables that filled the lower terrace. They formed a close group and I manoeuvred myself within earshot of their voluble conversations. It was time to start using the Yashica and as the elaborate pavilions provided endless scope and angles for photography I had plenty of excuse to linger. However, I was careful not to include any members of the trade party in my pictures. Some of the Japanese security men mingling with the crowds were obvious, and I guessed that there were others who were not. I didn't want anyone to haul me to one side and start with the third degree.

The Chinese were talking freely, confident that the swarms of Japanese on all sides would not understand them. They talked mostly in the Peking dialect, which was unfortunate although it was something I should have expected. I am much more fluent in Mandarin and Cantonese.

I counted twenty-nine members of the party, all male ranging in age from the early thirties to the late fifties. They had six Japanese guide-hosts, three of them attractive young women who were explaining the history and artistic merits of the buildings around us. It was all very cosy and the Chinese were smiling and enjoying themselves. After the dull round of factories they had endured it was understandable.

I trailed in their wake as they moved

up the next flight of steps to the Yomeimon Gate, the famous Gate of Sunlight, the name implying that a visitor could stand entranced by its beauty for as long as daylight lasted. It stood upon cream-lacquered pillars and was dazzling with gold leaf and decoration. Every beam-end was carved into a dragon's head. On either side of the gateway were beautiful panels in black and green and blue, decorated with peacocks and doves, flowers and leaves and branches.

Again I clicked the Yashica enthusiastically while I strained my ears to pick out fragments of intelligible speech from the massed babble of a score of Chinese voices.

Fifteen minutes passed before the delegates passed through the Yomeimon Gate and by that time my interest had been narrowed down to two of their number. All the others were stimulated by the shrine, taking photographs, asking questions and chattering with excitement. The two exceptions were watchful and silent. They were part of the group and yet they were distant. They did not mix and they did not smile. I had heard them address each other briefly and learned that their names were Shang and Hu.

Shang was the tallest man of the group. He had a sour and sallow face with sharp slitted eyes and a mouth that was as friendly as a steel trap. His colleague Hu was a few inches shorter, but probably weighed in at the same level around a hundred-and-ninety pounds. His face was sullen and bloated, shrinking his eyes to a deep, pig-like glitter behind folds of flesh. I knew instinctively that these two were the watchdogs, the high level security men sent to ensure that the good party members did not disgrace themselves or defect.

The same instinct also told me that if any members of the trade delegation were involved in any murky side issues of crime or espionage, then it was more likely to be the security men than the

121

average trade and economics experts. Anything deceitful or vicious would be in their line of business.

I followed them through to the Karamon Gate, the last gateway before the silver grey roofs of the Toshogu Shrine. It was a smaller gateway, exquisitely designed in Chinese style in cream and black and gold. The delegates rushed to it, but Shang and Hu held back. They turned their heads and looked at me with direct, appraising stares.

I gave them the vague smile of an embarrassed stranger and then walked past at a tangent to photograph the carved screen panels beside the gateway. However, I was still acutely conscious of their dark, burning gaze. I could feel it like a magnified double beam of malevolence on a spot midway between my shoulder blades. For a few seconds my skin was alive with nameless crawling things that were invisible and ice cold. I wanted to shudder. I wondered if I could possibly have aroused their suspicions and yet I was certain that I was no more conspicuous than any of the hordes of amateur photographers who flocked around the shrine.

After a few minutes I turned back to the Karamon Gate. Shang and Hu had joined the rest of the trade delegation and were passing through to the shrine and the tomb of Ieyasu beyond. They were no longer paying me any attention. I waited for the gateway to clear and then received a sudden shock.

Among the visitors on the far side of the gateway was a young woman in a rich blue silk *kimono* with a pure white sash. The dress caught my eye and then I saw her face. For a split second our eyes met as the path cleared between us.

I recognized Kukiko.

Before I could step forward the space between us was again blocked. A large party of Japanese schoolgirls had been politely waiting for the Chinese to move on. Now their teachers led them forward to congregate in a well-drilled swarm of neat navy blue uniforms around the Karamon Gate. Over their heads I saw Kukiko turn quickly away.

For a few seconds I hesitated, uncertain whether to continue after the Chinese or give chase to the girl. Then I decided that to push rudely through the dense mass of schoolgirls might attract attention and so I chose Kukiko. I moved in a circle to head her off but she reached the great Sunlight Gate before me and trotted quickly down to the lower terrace. I followed without any undue haste.

I saw her immediately. She had stopped beside one of the many uniformed policemen who were stationed around the shrines and she was talking and smiling boldly. For an instant I thought that she was about to point me out as an undesirable threat, but then I realized that she was faking an enquiry simply to gain the unwitting protection of the policeman. She seemed confident that I would not approach her while she kept his company.

I was tempted to walk up and betray her as a girl *Yakusa*, but reluctantly I had to put the temptation aside. Even if I was believed there would be endless questions and delays, my own presence here would need an explanation, and I would lose the only opportunity I was likely to have of staying close and eavesdropping on the Chinese.

I looked for Shino and any of his known friends, but there were no more familiar faces. Kukiko appeared to be alone except for the favoured policeman whom she was still holding in blithe conversation. I had to re-think my strategy and rather than waste more time I returned to the upper terrace.

The schoolgirls had passed through the Karamon Gate, but I was forced to linger there and take a few phogoraphs to maintain my cover. There was a policeman on duty who had already given me a curious look when I had moved after Kukiko. Tourist behaviour followed definite patterns and I could not afford too many deviations from the norm.

The Chinese were returning from the tomb behind the shrine. I waited for them and concentrated my camera on every angle of the gorgeous vermilion temple with its gilded wealth of precious metals and inspired art. Set amongst majestic trees at the head of the valley it was the final culmination of all the glory of Buddhist and Shinto architecture that had preceded it.

When the Chinese departed I tagged on again, deciding that I could risk giving the actual tomb of Ieyasu a miss. There was more to see in the form of shrines and the tomb of the grandson of the great *Shogun*, and although I had to move ahead or behind the trade delegation between stops I contrived to be close at each site where there was something to admire and photograph.

I overheard a multitude of scraps of talk, but nothing that was of any obvious value. The culture vultures among the comrades were comparing

Nikko to Peking, and commenting on Chinese influence on the Japanese treasures. The others were talking generally and when the tour was over they touched briefly on the trade bonds they were here to cement. One pair discussed an electronics factory they had studied in Nagoya, but to my frustration no mention was made of their visit to the Koga car company in Osaka.

As our wandering progressed I kept a wary eye open for a blue *kimono*, but Kukiko had either removed herself altogether or she was careful to keep out of my sight. I saw no more of her, and nothing of any of her known *Yakusa* associates.

The Chinese finally led me back down the cedar avenues to the parking lot, and by then I had decided that my visit to Nikko had been a waste of time. I let them depart ahead of me and noticed that Shang and Hu climbed into one of the official cars instead of joining the main delegation in the big tourist coach.

I knew they were all scheduled to return to a late luncheon at their hotel in Nikko where I could not follow them, and so I sat thoughtful for a few minutes in my hired Datsun. I toyed with the idea of returning to the shrines to make a more determined search for Kukiko, but now that she was alert to my presence I doubted that I would find her. Finally I started the engine and drove the Datsun slowly back towards Nikko.

As I crossed the River Daiya I was still thinking hard, but before I reached the far end of the bridge all my thoughts were swept away. I saw a black car flash past heading west, away from Nikko, and I saw briefly the sour, sallow face at the wheel. It was Shang, and the man half hidden beside him was Hu.

I swung the Datsun automatically in pursuit.

They were headed out on the hairpin-curved Irohazaka Driveway, a superb mountain road that swept up in a series of great climbing loops into the heart of the Nikko national park. I stayed a couple of bends behind but kept them in sight above me. The black car was a powerful cruiser but did not seem to be in any undue hurry on the open road. I thought dubiously that perhaps even Shang and Hu had souls that could appreciate the rugged mountain scenery.

Twice I glanced down and saw a lavender blue Koga 1000 on the bends below, although at first I thought that it had only registered because I had become familiar with the new pastel colours and the model of the car.

After eight miles the road dropped again to the shores of Lake Chuzenji at the foot of the overshadowing bulk of Mount Nantai. The lake was sparkling blue in the afternoon sun, seen through a riot of pink blossom on the plum trees that lined the lakeside road. At the bottom of the mountain there was another temple shrine and I saw the black car pulled up at the roadside. Shang and Hu were entering the shrine and I put my foot down to speed past them, turning my head and hiding my face to look out over the lake.

I parked two hundred yards along the road, climbed out and started to walk back. That was when the lavender blue Koga shot past. The girl driver was not wearing a blue *kimono* but it was Kukiko.

She passed out of sight and again I stood undecided. Then I resolved to concentrate on the two Chinese and continued towards the shrine. In the temple grounds I spotted Shang and Hu passing through a gateway on the far side that led on to a pathway ascending the mountain. I didn't want to get too close and was almost grateful to the white-robed Shinto priest who delayed me with a visitors book that had to be signed by all climbers on the mountain. Shang and Hu had already signed and I added a fictitious Japanese name.

The mountain was thickly wooded and the steep path was stepped with branches wedged horizontally. A crisp carpet of dried brown leaves lay everywhere underfoot although overhead the new spring buds were forming on the branches. I climbed up slowly through tall pines, cedars and silver birch, listening frequently for sounds from the two men above me. They were making no attempt to move in silence and so I was able to stay out of sight and follow the sounds of their progress.

As I climbed higher the lake appeared in flashes of blue through the treetops below. After an hour I reached a gravel road that circled round the mountain and here I had to pause. Shang and Hu were walking up the road a hundred yards ahead of me, apparently soaking up the sunshine and admiring the magnificent scenery all round. After another hundred yards they turned off the road and again followed the direct path up the mountain.

I moved through the trees, avoiding the road except for the few seconds that it took to sprint across when I got level with the continuing path. There I stopped again, listening for sounds from above. I heard the crack of a twig and the swish of leaves which sounded a safe distance away, but before I moved on I glanced back along the gravel road.

I saw Kukiko climb up on to the road from the first leg of the path. She was wearing jeans and a black sweater and stood for a moment to regain her breath. The recurring conflict of decision surfaced again, but again the Chinese won. I continued up the new path in their wake, but with more caution now that I knew that I was also being followed.

The new path soon became much steeper, leading up a straight gulley that looked like a scar slashed down the mountainside by a savage storm. It was full of loose rocks and boulders and the black and white splintered hulks of dead, uprooted trees. I climbed for another hour, keeping low and making use of all the available cover. Several times I saw glimpses of Shang and Hu climbing a few hundred feet above me, and I knew that if I was not careful there must also be moments when I would be visible from above or below. I saw nothing more of Kukiko which meant that she too was feeling her way with utmost secrecy.

The long gulley became almost vertical and choked with huge boulders. The trail of dead trees came to an end and the dark green pines that wooded the slopes on either side closed in to strangle the ascending dirt path. I began to encounter patches of half-melted snow, and then frozen drifts. Nantai was eight thousand feet high and the ascent was a walk through the seasons: there was autumn in the dead leaves, spring in the air, summer in the sunshine, and winter on the final slopes.

After three hours of climbing I was

close to the top, moving up another gulley of dull red dirt littered with red lava rocks. Every step I made was slow and wary and my instinct for self-preservation was working overtime. The mountain was silent and for the past ten minutes I had neither seen nor heard any movement from Shang or Hu. I did not know whether I had missed them or whether they were hidden somewhere and lying in wait for me.

I reached the summit and looked out over a vast valley to the pine and snow covered slopes of more mountains far away. I was alone and exposed and every sense and nerve-end urged me to get back under cover. I ducked and turned as I looked back down the mountain and it was then that the first shot rang out in the icy stillness.

I felt the wind of the bullet and now there was no more doubt in my mind that Shang and Hu were trying to kill me.

8

IT had been obvious right from the start that there could only be two possible reasons for Shang and Hu to have climbed Mount Nantai. They would not have left the members of the trade delegation without supervision simply for the pure physical pleasure of the excursion. The answer had to be either a rendezvous with a third party, or a deliberate attempt to decoy and ambush an interfering private investigator. I had believed that there was no way they could have known my name, my face or my business, and so the trailing presence of Kukiko had led me to hope for a rendezvous. Now I knew that I was wrong and that Shang and Hu had lured me here to die.

Shang had risen to his feet from behind a red volcanic boulder fifty feet below me. Behind him was Lake

Chuzenji like a distant, misshapen blue disc that was squeezed in the middle with range upon range of low mountains beyond. He had his revolver levelled for a second shot which cracked behind me as I bounded away along the crest of the summit.

My instinct was to dive down into that deep valley on the far side but mercifully my brain was double-thinking to override the impulse. I stayed on top, crouching low and moving fast, and the third angry bullet came up from those snow-bound north slopes where I should logically have sought safety. A quick glance over my right shoulder showed the heavier bulk of Hu scrambling quickly upward through the low ranks of young fir trees.

I was unarmed and cornered on the summit by two ruthless and determined men with revolvers, but I was running on near level ground while Shang and Hu were still struggling on the steep north and south slopes. They were moving east to cut me off in a pincer movement but when I reached the point where I had to plunge downward I was leading the race.

A dozen miles away were the sprawling, unhospital grey-streaked flanks of the next mountain and I made a virtually suicidal dive into the great gulf of empty space that intervened. In my job it was necessary to be physically active to stay alive and back in Hong Kong I spent many hours in Sunny Cheong's gymnasium, practising hand stands, cartwheels, judo bouts and working the parallel bars. Now I put it all to the test and performed the most reckless series of flying cartwheels I had ever attempted down the rugged east slope of Nantai.

By all the laws of chance I should at least have broken my neck. The east slope was a wasteland of ice patches, snow drifts, boulders and small trees. My wrists and ankles took a savage pounding as I spun downwards but miraculously not a bone snapped. The risk was justified by the fact that both Shang and Hu were shooting wildly at my cartwheeling figure as I hurtled between them. They were shouting angrily as they ran forward but the speed of my performance had taken them both by surprise.

That same speed should have killed me. Once started there was no way I could check my violent descent except to aim for the largest snow drift in my path. I could only pray that it concealed nothing solid for the last of my nightmare revolutions threw me into the great pile of heaped snow like a runaway space wheel sucked down by the fearsome pull of gravity.

When I went through the icy crust I felt as though I had smashed into a plate glass window. Then I was ploughing through the soft centre and out the other side in a sliding avalanche of snow and rolling boulders. I had no more control of my own momentum and direction but at least my rate of fall had been slowed. Before it could pick up again my body hit the first of the miniature pine trees that dotted the upper slopes and was bashed from tree to tree. Some of them snapped and some simply sprang upright again as I rolled over them, but they brought me to a skidding halt on the frozen, steeply angled earth.

I was aware that I was hurt, there was pain in my ankle, a bruised ache in my ribs and blood dripping from a deep gash in the heel of my hand. However, I was also aware that Shang and Hu were still closing in for the kill. They were above me now, descending fast but retaining their sanity. A revolver cracked again and another bullet smashed snow from the laden branches of the nearest fir tree.

I lurched to my feet and set off in a downhill run that was nearly as desperate as flinging myself bodily from the top of the mountain. I reached the next belt of trees that were shoulder high and ducked for cover with more bullets buzzing like hot wasps around my ears. I stumbled on an ice patch and pain stabbed up sharply from my already weakened ankle. I knew then that I had sprained it badly and there was a limit to how far I could hope to run.

I limped deeper into the trees. My ankle folded up beneath me as my foot twisted over a root and I fell and slithered another dozen feet. I scrambled up again and continued headlong. Shang and Hu were crashing noisily through the trees behind me. I found another deep gulley that slashed and zig-zagged its way down the mountainside and slid into it. Boulders and more dead trees choked every yard of the way but there was plenty of cover and that was what I needed now. The sounds of pursuit told me that the two Chinese were fast catching me up.

I squeezed between the jumbles of grey rocks, searching for a crack into which I could crawl and hide. There was nothing and I could feel my heart hammering like a pneumatic road drill.

My chest was heaving and my mouth was dry. My ankle refused to take my weight any further and I dropped down to a crawl. I covered ten yards and then heard a sibilant hissing sound that made my blood freeze. I thought it was a snake coiled in the heap of brushwood that was jammed under a fallen tree and started to twist away. In that moment a slim white hand reached out through a gap between the dead branches and gripped my shoulder.

"In here," Kukiko whispered softly, and I realized that the first hissing noise had been her warning to silence.

She arched her back, lifting the blanket of brushwood, and I crawled thankfully into the cramped hollow beside her. The branches dropped back into place and I felt sharp twigs sticking into me from every angle except my right side where Kukiko pressed close against me. The hand that had touched my shoulder now moved discreetly to cover my mouth.

We huddled together, hardly daring

to breathe, and with an effort of will I controlled my lung-bursting need to gulp down loud draughts of air. My heart was thudding violently, but I convinced myself that I was the only one who could actually hear it.

We heard Shang and Hu searching on either side of the ravine above our heads. I guessed that from their vantage points they would see anything that moved at our level and so we both remained perfectly motionless. Slowly the sounds moved away as the two men worked their way down the mountain. There was silence, but five minutes passed before Kukiko removed her hand from my mouth.

"You are fortunate, David Chan," she said quietly. "If they had caught you they would have killed you."

"I'm grateful for your help," I answered sincerely.

She smiled and then lifted the screen of branches and crawled out into the open. She stood up to stretch her limbs and pick the twigs and dead leaves from her clothes and her hair. I followed more slowly and used a boulder to pull myself upright. Kukiko inspected herself for scratches and then made an anxious fuss over my cut hand. I gave her my handkerchief to use as a bandage. When she had tied the knot she became more worried about Shang and Hu and looked down the mountainside.

"The Chinese may return," she decided. "If they have realized that your foot is hurt they will know that you cannot have got far. We must move from here."

I didn't argue. She helped me to climb out of the gulley and then took my arm around her shoulders. We moved clumsily across the face of the mountain, circling round toward the western slopes. It was dusk and the shadows were lengthening in the valleys. Lake Chuzenji was no longer blue but a dull grey. By the time we felt safe from Shang and Hu and began to descend it was dark.

We were both weary when we found the stream. My foot was throbbing furiously and Kukiko was floundering as she struggled to support my weight. I calculated that we were down to the level of the road but we were hopelessly lost among tall pine and beech trees, and silver birches that loomed like crooked ghosts. Kukiko had lost her sense of direction and most of the stars were blotted out by the treetops and cloud.

"We'll rest until dawn," I told her. "It's pointless to hobble about all night. We don't even know where we're going."

She let me down without protest and I eased off my shoe and let my sprained right ankle dangle in the ice cold stream. It made me gasp but I knew that I would have to bathe it repeatedly unless I wanted to be incapacitated for several days. Kukiko huddled down beside me. She was shivering and I put an arm around her shoulders.

After we had rested there was time for talk. All the questions that I had been forced to put aside could now be asked and I was especially curious to know why she had helped me.

"If the Chinese want you dead, then perhaps it is important that you stay alive," she answered cautiously.

"But once your friends wanted me dead," I reminded her. "Shino went to great pains to fake my suicide in the path of the bullet express!"

"That was a mistake. I realize now that you are not what we believed you to be."

"You mean an agent of the Chinese?"

"Yes."

"When I saw you at the Toshogu Shrine, and again here on the mountain, I thought that you must be a friend of the Chinese."

She smiled faintly in the darkness. "When I saw you in these places I continued to think the same — until

I saw them try to kill you."

I tightened my arm around her. The night air was bitterly cold and the intimacy was approved.

"Kukiko," I said softly. "Why were you at the shrine? And why are you here on the mountain?"

"Perhaps for the same reason as you. I was watching the Chinese?"

"Why should the *Yakusa* watch the Chinese? What makes your people think that the trade delegation can have had anything to do with the disappearance of Tony Fallon?"

She frowned and tightened her lips. "When you speak of the *Yakusa* you speak of things that must not be said. I cannot say any more."

I didn't push her for a moment. Instead I endured the torture of dipping my foot back into the icy flow of the stream. Thirty seconds was enough and then I gently rubbed it dry with the sleeve of my jacket.

"Have you ever met Tony Fallon?"

"No — and you must not ask me

any more questions. It is best if you do not ask anyone. It would be much better for you to return home to Hong Kong."

"Is that a word of friendly advice from Kukiko? Or a threat from the *Yakusa*?"

"It is both," she conceded honestly. "As soon as it is possible you should say *sayonara* to Japan."

Her eyes were serious and her tone was final. She had pulled away from me but after a moment of silence she moved close again. Each of us needed the body heat of the other, for on a night like this enemies would freeze of exposure. I realized also that I was hungry, and nothing would have been more welcome than a bowl of hot soup. The stream gurgled darkly at our feet, but I would have to be very thirsty before I chilled my belly with that.

I sensed that Kukiko was feeling the same discomforts, and also that she was afraid. I could feel her body tense every time a nightbird flapped its wings, and there were enough nocturnal creaks and rustles to make me wonder whether bears and wolves still roamed on Nantai. It seemed best to keep talking, if only to keep her mind from the terrors of the night, and so I renewed the conversation with a new variation on an old theme.

"Kukiko is both beautiful and intelligent," I complimented her softly. "So why does she support gangsters like the *Yakusa*?"

She was not slow to defend her friends. "The *Yakusa* are not gangsters. Only our enemies call us that. Once Japan was ruled by the *Daimyo*, the feudal lords who lived in the great castles and were very cruel to the common people. In those days the only help for the peasants were the wandering warriors who would dedicate their hearts and their swords for a noble cause. We called them *Samurai*. Today we have the *Zaibatsu*, and the pressures of American capitalism and Asian communism that are all trying to exploit the people and smother the old Japan. The *Yakusa* is the heart of old Japan, and we are the new *Samurai*."

"But the *Yakusa* operate on the proceeds of crime and extortion."

"You know very little, David Chan. The *Yakusa* only extort from the wealthy, from those who have already stolen from the people. We have influence on every level, but most *Yakusa* are peasant born. We are the people. Go into any working class area in Tokyo or Osaka and you will find that the people do not have any great faith in the government, in the police, or in the *Zaibatsu* factories that own and employ them. They trust only the *Yakusa*."

"Then why does the *Yakusa* take orders from the *Zaibatsu* — from Mister Shinjira?"

She stared at me angrily. "The *Yakusa* does not take orders from Mister Shinjira. And you are asking bad questions again."

"I am sorry," I apologized. "There

are still so many things that I do not understand."

"Then understand this. There is good and bad in everything, even *Zaibatsu* and *Yakusa*. Therefore it is not impossible for *Zaibatsu* and *Yakusa* to have common cause. If a factory closes then jobs are lost. Nobody gains."

That was the only solid hint she had given me, and it was as much as she dared. I sensed that she regretted the words as soon as she had spoken and she would say no more. When I asked further questions she simply advised me again to leave Japan.

★ ★ ★

By dawn we were stiff with cold and as soon as it was possible we began to move. The slanted angle of the first dim grey shafts of light told us that east was behind the shoulder of the mountain, and so I calculated that the course of the stream should lead us back to the road and the lake.

My foot was still painful but spartan ice water treatment ha prevented the ankle from swelling an I had strapped it up with a sleeve from my shirt. Kukiko supported some of my weight but I limped beside her more easily than the night before. The terrain was rough but reasonably level as we circled the base of Nantai. We warmed with the exercise and the increasing power of the sun. Birds warbled in the dappled branches and the stream glinted and tumbled merrily through the forest. With a pretty girl on my arm it was almost a pleasure stroll, although we were tired and relieved when we finally reached the road.

We walked back through the small town of Chuzenji until the blue sparkle of the lake appeared again through the pink screens of blossom. Then Kukiko stopped.

"Wait here," she advised. "If there is more trouble then you cannot run. It is best if I go ahead and make sure

...hinese are not waiting near

...le sense, and because we
... so close and intimate all
...ough the night I had almost forgotten
that we were not on exactly the
same side.

"Mine is the red Datsun," I told her.
And I allowed her to help me over to
a bench seat that the town council of
Chuzenji had obligingly provided to
overlook the beauties of the lake.

Kukiko hurried away along the
lakeside.

Five minutes later the lavender blue
Koga 1000 flashed past in the direction
of Nikko. Her smile was just as fleeting
as she waved goodbye and I realized
that Kukiko had abandoned me.

9

I HOBBLED to my car and checked that it had not been primed to explode in my face. Then I got inside, started the engine and drove thoughtfully to Nikko. When I arrived I went shopping for a new shirt, a strong crepe bandage for my sprained ankle and a tin of elastoplast for my gashed hand. There was no sign of the big tour coach outside the hotel where the Chinese trade delegation had stayed, but I knew they were scheduled to return to Osaka. Neither was there any sign of the lavender blue Koga and I guessed that Kukiko was also on her way home. There was nothing to be gained by prolonging my pangs of thirst and hunger so I spent an hour in a restaurant before following the circus.

Ten miles south of Nikko I got

lucky. I passed a couple of European hitch-hikers on the roadside, two of the bearded, shoe-string tourists who flooded the main roads of the east. I picked them up and checked that one of them possessed an international driving licence before inviting him to take the wheel. I was able to rest my foot for the remainder of the drive to Tokyo and the time passed swiftly enough. My passengers were students who spoke good English and chatted amiably about their travels.

We parted two hours later outside Tokyo Main Station and I drove the last short lap into Ginza.

Ken Kenichi was surprised to see me, or perhaps he was surprised by my battered appearance, it was difficult to tell. Most people can see their own faults more clearly in others, and one of the things I found most disconcerting about the Japanese was that their faces were often as bland and uninformative as my own. Kenichi showed concern over my limp and taped hand, and the whisky bottle came out again as he begged me earnestly to explain.

I gave him a full account of what had happened and at the same time I watched his face. He frowned repeatedly and I began to wonder if he was frowning too often.

"Somehow you must have aroused the suspicions of these two men," he said at last.

"Perhaps, but I do not think they would have made an immediate decision to eliminate me on suspicion alone. It is more likely they recognized my face and knew something of my reasons for following them." I made a delicate pause.

"This means someone must have reported your movements and given them your description." Kenichi spoke carefully and his eyes did not waver from my own. "The Chinese were warned."

"That is my conclusion also. I do not know whether to suspect Mister Shinjira, the girl Naoka, or my own

155

client." It would have been crude to add the name of Ken Kenichi, but we both knew it was there.

"You have forgotten the *Yakusa*," he said slowly.

"That is not logical. Nothing would have been easier for Kukiko than to hand me over to Shang and Hu. I was virtually crippled and they were only yards away. Instead she helped me to escape."

"The big *Yakusa* gangs can count their members in thousands," Kenichi informed me. "In an organization of that size it is rare for more than a few high ranking individual members to know anything of the overall strategy. The girl had one task to perform. Perhaps your friend Shino, or Morita, had another. The girl may have acted on her own initiative and blundered."

"It is a possibility," I agreed politely.

I drank some of his whisky and continued to watch his face. He remained without expression. I had not asked him directly if he had betrayed me, and so he could pretend that he did not know what was in my mind. An open book did not have to be read aloud, its meaning was clear to any discerning eye.

"One fact has been proved," Kenichi said at last. "You were right to believe that the Chinese are in some way involved. If they were not then they would not have tried to kill you."

I smiled faintly. "From that point of view I have gained something from my trip to Nikko. But it is very limited progress. I still don't know where to find Tony Fallon, or why he visited Koga cars. If anything the whole mystery is even more complicated than before."

Kenichi made his fingers into a steeple and rested his arms on his desk. It was a habit he had adopted as a lawyer and one that would probably stay with him for the rest of his life. He gazed at me steadily.

"David, I have taken a new interest in this investigation of yours. It has prompted me to do some research into the background of Mister Shinjira and the Koga car company. Mister Shinjira still emerges as above suspicion, but I have learned something that may or may not be relevant about Koga cars. As you may know, industrial espionage has been rife in Japan over the past few years, and Koga cars has been a victim to this sort of activity."

"How?" Anything was worth following up so I gave him some encouragement.

"Six months ago Koga planned a big sales drive for their new Koga 1000. A lot of money was spent in preparing the promotion and advertizing campaign. Two weeks before it was due to be launched one of their chief rivals beat them to the punch with a campaign for their own new model using practically the same selling slogans, the same film ideas, the same camera backgrounds for the glossy brochures. It was identical to the planned Koga material, and of course Koga had to abandon their sales drive until they could think up a whole batch of new ideas. It put them months behind and cost millions of yen."

"So somebody at Koga has been selling secrets to rival car firms."

"Precisely. It may not have any connection with this present case, but on the other hand it may be a point worth remembering."

Or it may be an elaborate smoke-screen I thought wryly, although it would have been ungracious to have voiced the thought aloud.

"Were there any repercussions within the Koga car company?" I asked the question merely to show interest. "Any dismissals? Or any dark clouds of suspicion on any particular heads?"

"No doubt they held their own witch-hunt, but there is no evidence that the culprit was ever found."

We were silent for a moment. Kenichi drank his whisky but I noticed that he did not throw it back with one swallow. It was a departure from his normal behaviour, but it did not necessarily signify anything, except that he was prolonging the drink to gain thinking time. When he had finished he poured us both another.

"I have a second item of information," he said casually as he pushed my glass across the desk. He put the bottle away before he continued: "You are not the only foreign devil in Japan who is searching for the mysterious Tony Fallon. While you have been visiting Nikko there has been another stranger asking questions here in Tokyo."

I stared at him. "Who is this man?"

Kenichi shrugged. "An American who gave his name as Robert Baxter. That is all I know."

"He came here to you?"

"No, he has been making his own enquiries."

"How do you know?"

Kenichi showed his teeth in a confident smile. "I received a telephone call, from a director of another car factory here in Tokyo. When I made my initial enquiries after Fallon on your instructions I called at most of the factories which he might logically have visited in the normal process of his job. As it happened that line of investigation proved a blank and I eventually traced him through the hotel address you were able to give me. However, when this American called yesterday asking virtually the same questions, this particular director remembered my visit. He is an acquaintance with whom I have sometimes played golf, and so he gave me a courtesy call to let me know what was happening."

I was frowning now, for the diversity of dedicated searchers for Tony Fallon was confusing enough, without the addition of yet another unknown quality.

"Are you sure that Robert Baxter gave only his name? And no indications of why he was looking for Fallon?"

Kenichi looked bland. "I could find out."

It was an offer and abruptly I decided to take it up. If there was an American named Baxter moving into the case, then Kenichi should easily be able to

161

track the man down on his own ground. And if Baxter did not exist, if he was just another subterfuge to waste my time or distract my attention, then it would be a smart move to throw him back to his author. I adopted a suitably worried look and stated my problem.

"Ken, I have to get back to Osaka. The trade delegation has returned there and I'm sure that Kukiko must have followed them. Osaka has to be the focal point for this case, and also I'm not happy at leaving Sharon Vale alone in Kyoto only a few miles away. But at the same time this American could be important." I looked at him hopefully. "I can't be in two places at once, but Tokyo is your city. You could find Robert Baxter for me."

"Yes. I can do this for you. At my usual daily fee and expenses." His smile was unperturbed, which meant that Robert Baxter could be genuine, or that Ken Kenichi was too clever to show any adverse reaction at being neatly foiled.

I showed relief. "Thank you, Ken. That takes one weight off my shoulders. When you get results you can telephone me at the Kyoto Tower Hotel."

"I will do that." Kenichi nodded calmly. "But before you return to Kyoto you must join me for a meal. There is a restaurant on the ground floor of this building which serves excellent *sukiyaki*!"

It was another offer I couldn't refuse. To have done so would have caused great offence, and even though I didn't know yet whether he had had any part in the attempt to kill me, there was nothing positive to be gained from acting like a mannerless barbarian.

When I finally left for Kyoto it was after a satisfying luncheon and a couple of bottles of warmed *saki*. Kenichi had been an affable host, but by tacit agreement we had dropped the subject of business and talked of other things. We had parted friends with a handshake, and on Kenichi's part a slight bow. Behind the wheel of the red Datsun once again I had plenty of time to think, but thought alone could not create the answers I needed.

I looked for more hitch-hikers but on this leg of the journey there was no one to relieve me from driving. Fortunately the Datsun needed only a light pressure on the accelerator and I drove carefully to ensure that I did not have to make any violent stabs at the brake pedal. The crepe bandage gave good support to my injured ankle, and although the drive down took an hour longer than the trip up it did not cause me too much discomfort.

I stopped at a roadhouse just beyond Toyohashi for coffee and a sandwich, and it was dark when I drove on through the ugly sprawl of Nagoya. The frequent glare of approaching headlights made me realize that I was very tired and it was a relief when I finally drove through the familiar green hills and down into the great bowl of fairy lights that was Kyoto.

When I entered the hotel I was

tempted to go straight to my room and sleep, but first I had to call on Sharon Vale. I tidied myself in the elevator and then knocked on her door.

She appeared promptly. It was only ten o'clock but she was wearing a knee-length, pink-flowered housecoat over her nightdress. Her golden hair was gloriously loose and she looked at me as though I was the prodigal son returned.

"David, I've been wondering what on earth has happened to you. I expected you back this morning."

"There were some complications." I apologized as I closed the door.

"Next time I'm coming with you," she told me firmly. "I'm getting damned tired of just sitting around this hotel room while you investigate. And don't tell me again that it could be dangerous to accompany you. Nothing could be worse than dying of boredom and worry. I didn't come here to take a permanent back seat."

"When we came here we didn't know

what was involved."

"That's all very well, but — " She was warming up nicely but suddenly she noticed my limp and the wide strip of elastoplast across the palm of my hand. Her frustration was swamped by a flood of concern and she rushed to help me.

"David, you *have* hurt yourself again!"

"Only superficial damage," I assured her. But I allowed her to fuss over me and steer me into a chair."

"You look worn out," she observed. "And I'll bet you need a drink."

"I've done a lot of driving over the past three days, with a sleepless night and a lot of hectic acrobatics in between."

She brought me a scotch and sat on the arm of my chair. It was very cosy and the housecoat had fallen away from her bare thigh. I made an effort to concentrate on the scotch.

"Tell me what happened," she insisted.

"I spent yesterday following the Red Chinese trade delegation as I planned. It all seemed to be a waste of time — until the two security men with the group led me a dance up a mountain and tried to make sure that I didn't come down." I looked up at her baffled face and saw that it wasn't enough. Wearily I went into full details.

She was shocked and still mystified. "It doesn't make sense, David. First the *Yakusa* tried to murder you, and now this girl saves your life."

"They do appear to have confusing principles," I agreed. "Yamamoto compared them to the American Mafia, while Kukiko describes them as a bunch of Japanese Robin Hoods. I suppose it all depends on your point of view."

She played nervously with the belt of her housecoat. "This makes two different groups of people who have tried to kill you," she said slowly. "The *Yakusa* and the Chinese. But why, David? What has all this got to do with Tony? I don't understand it."

"Try another mystery for size," I suggested gently. "What do you know about an American named Robert Baxter?"

She looked totally blank. "Nothing. Who is he?"

"I don't know yet. He could be anything, from the real Mafia to the F.B.I. All know is that it's open season on your lost fiance, and Robert Baxter is joining in the hunt. He's been asking questions in Tokyo."

She stared at me for a moment but I kept my expression blank. Finally she got up and poured herself a drink. She kept her back toward me so I couldn't see her face.

"This man Baxter — was he from Detroit?"

"He could be. Are you expecting somebody from Detroit?"

"No."

"But that's where this all started."

"No, David!" She turned sharply and her face was angry, as though I had tried to take an unfair advantage. "It started in Japan — when Tony went missing."

"So who is Robert Baxter?"

Sharon shrugged her shoulders helplessly while her fingers twisted the belt of her housecoat. I felt certain she had not recognized the name, but she was obviously disturbed by the thought of another visitor from America taking part in the search for Tony Fallon.

10

I AWOKE the next morning after a good, long sleep and felt fit and refreshed. Most of my aches and pains had gone and I could walk normally, although I decided to retain the crepe bandage for support. I showered and shaved and then dressed in a light brown suit with a cream shirt and a wine red tie. It was the last of the three suits I had packed for my trip to Japan, and I hoped that it would fare better than the others which were beyond repair.

While I made myself presentable I had more time to think, and again my mind retraced all the old steps like a blind man moving up and down the same paths in a vain search for something he had lost. The facts paraded in slow review and I re-examined them from the beginning.

Tony Fallon had come to Japan. His reasons were unknown. He had paid a visit to the Koga car factory — but again his reasons were unknown. Instead of staying in Osaka, where he had friends and contacts, he had chosen to study in Kyoto, at the *Yushimaso Ryokan*. According to the testimony of Mister Sato he had left the *ryokan* in good spirits, dressed for an evening of pleasure, presumably with our delightful friend Naoka. According to Naoka he had not appeared at their rendezvous. Now nearly two weeks had passed and no one had seen him since. Those were the bare facts, and all my gallivanating around Japan had added little to them.

Except that I was not the only one looking for the invisible man, and at least two of the competing groups were prepared to kill me to keep me out of their way.

After my thoughts had run themselves into a rut I pushed Tony Fallon out of my mind and concentrated on the equally familiar paths surrounding my trip to Nikko. Someone had tipped off the Chinese and I ran a mental check over everyone involved. Starting with the least likely there was Inspector Yamamoto, who had my full signed statement on why I was here and detailing everything up to the point where I had narrowly missed being sliced up into Japanese chop suey by the wheels of the bullet express.

Then there was Mister Sato, the manager of the *Yushimaso Ryokan*. He was a guileless little man with glasses and an endearing smile. He had answered my questions frankly and had unhesitatingly showed me the room where Fallon had stayed, with Fallon's suitcase still awaiting his return in the corner. Needless to say the room and the suitcase had revealed nothing helpful. Somehow I couldn't rate Mister Sato as a villain in disguise, but he was a man who could be used or frightened. Those points were worth bearing in mind.

Next there was Mister Shinjira, but I had a strong suspicion that it was Shinjira who had forewarned the *Yakusa*, and as the *Yakusa* and the Chinese appeared to be in opposition it was illogical to suspect Shinjira again.

Since the episode on Mount Nantai I had talked with both Sharon Vale and Ken Kenichi, and in each case their reactions had been inconclusive. Kenichi was too bland, worse, I conceded ruefully, than these tricky Eurasians. Sharon had hidden secrets but I could not guess what they were. With those two I had an open mind.

That left Naoka, the sweet siren who listened in on the office intercom, and played sexy variations of the tea ceremony while a Chinese tape recorder hummed a silent tune in the background. Naoka had approached me to fish for answers, and she could have lured an unsuspecting Tony Fallon to his fate.

I put the final touches to ensuring a perfect knot in my tie and decided that I could do worse than renew my investigation with Naoka. If nothing else I might get offered another cup of Japanese tea.

★ ★ ★

I shared a breakfast table with Sharon and when she again raised the matter of coming with me I had a new but equally valid excuse.

"This girl and Tony were rather intimate," I said tactfully. "I don't think she'll talk freely in your presence. And I couldn't blame you if you felt hostile towards her."

"You mean you think I'll get madly jealous and scratch her eyes out."

"I mean the atmosphere won't be right for gaining her confidence."

She looked at me doubtfully, but she wasn't the only one who could play the innocent. Finally she was convinced and nodded.

"Alright, David. But the next time you leave this hotel I am definitely coming with you!"

I knew that I couldn't expect to find Naoka at home until the evening when she would finish work at the Koga car company and so it was late afternoon before I started out for Osaka. When I arrived I went first to the international telephone branch of the central post office and put a call through to Hong Kong.

That was another reason why I hadn't wanted Sharon along on this particular trip. During our last telephone conversation I had told Belinda not to call me back but to wait until I called her. The only return number I could have given would have been the Kyoto Tower Hotel, and things might have got awkward if Sharon had accepted a call on my behalf and learned that I was double-checking behind her back.

However, I was out of luck. There was no answer from the Chan Agency on the sixteenth floor of the skyscraper building overlooking Hong Kong harbour, which meant that both Belinda and Tracey were out. If there were any results to Belinda's trans-Pacific enquiries to Detroit then they would have to wait.

I went back to the Datsun and drove on to the apartment block. It was dark when I arrived and the street lamps threw pools of yellow light on the grey pavements. The apartment blocks themselves were vertical chessboards, the smaller white squares shaded by curtains. By a brief twist of the imagination the world was a cardboard facade with no depth. I wondered how true that might be of the regimented lives of the faithful company employees who inhabited this faceless rabbit warren, but then I shrugged the thought aside.

I had to concentrate on the problems I could solve — or so I hoped.

I got out of the Datsun and glanced upwards again. There was a light at Naoka's window which was promising.

I took the elevator up to the third floor, walked along the corridor and knocked on her door.

There was no answer.

I knocked again and waited. I could hear muffled voices from the other apartments along the corridor, a child laughing and a transistor radio blaring music, but from Naoka's door there was only silence.

A tiny ghost with prickly feet tip-toed up the back of my neck.

I tried the door handle and it turned smoothly. The door was not locked and as it cracked open I realized that the apartment was in darkness. The light I had seen from the street below had been put out. I gave the door a gentle push and stepped back and sideways as it swung inward.

Nothing happened. I eased inside for the light from the corridor showed that the miniature kitchen was empty. The door into the living room was open but I didn't let my silhouette show in the doorway. I stood to one side and reached one hand round for the light switch and clicked it down.

Again nothing happened. The click was very audible but the apartment remained in darkness.

Then I heard a soft girlish giggle.

"Naoka?" I whispered.

The giggle came again and I thought she was playing some schoolgirl trick. A figure moved in the gloom in the centre of the room.

Then light dazzled my eyes as a bulb was screwed home into the empty socket above her head. She wore a blue skirt with a white blouse and it took me two seconds to realize that it was not Naoka.

She had replaced the light bulb with her left hand, and in her right was the familiar little 0.32 automatic. She was smiling her familiar sweet smile.

It was Kukiko. Somehow, for all her faults, I didn't think she could smile and pull the trigger at the same time, so I didn't do anything hasty. I looked slowly around the apartment but only the flowers had been changed. The vase that had held the yellow chrysanthemums now displayed a carefully arranged spray of blue and white irises. Nothing else had been moved. The silk cushion that had concealed the tape recorder still leaned against the dividing screen, and I had the strange feeling that the tapes could still be turning.

"You can come in, Mister Chan," Kukiko said politely.

I stepped inside and slid the door shut behind me.

"Why the gun, Kukiko? The last time we met we were friends."

Her smile saddened a little. "The last time we met was on a mountain. We had mutual enemies, you were crippled, and there were no telephones. Now we are not on a mountain and our enemies have gone. And you are not crippled. I watched from the window as you got out of your car and walked into this building. You were not limping. You are a strong man, David Chan, and there are telephones in this building. You could hold me and call the police."

"You are cautious. Perhaps you are wise." I returned her smile. "But I can assure you the gun will not be necessary. I am still grateful for our friendship on the mountain."

She watched me for a moment. Then she chuckled softly as she lowered the gun. She called out a few brief words in Japanese.

I heard the sliding door move open behind me and turned my head. I found myself looking into the hot eyes of Toji. They glowered back at me from his gross moon face and he wasn't smiling. His eye-level was a few inches lower than my own, but his vast hulking body filled the whole width of the door frame. In fact he would have to turn sideways to get in. He wore the dark, double-breasted pinstripe suit and white polo-neck shirt of the *Yakusa*, but his tailor must have fitted him out in despair. He would

180

only have looked at home swinging through the trees in a fur coat.

I realized that he had been lurking outside, probably around the corner of the corridor, when I came in.

Kukiko spoke again. There was laughter in her tone but the words were an order.

The silent Toji gave me a hideous look, half threat and half a scowl of disappointment, and then he slid the door back between our faces. I decided I was glad Toji was an obedient soul and hoped that no one would ever give him the order he so obviously wanted.

I turned back to Kukiko and saw she was putting her baby automatic into her handbag. Her dark eyes twinkled.

"You are right, David Chan. The gun will not be necessary."

"I am offended," I told her sorrowfully, "To think you can only trust me while your pet *sumo* wrestler stands guard outside."

She looked hurt. In Japan to give

offense was the cardinal sin. "It is not always a precaution I would choose," she apologized.

"Where is your other friend, Shino?"

"Now you are giving offense. You are asking questions again."

It seemed that we were even but I risked losing more face and asked, "Where is Naoka?"

Apparently that was not such an offensive question for she merely shrugged and spread her hands. "She is not here."

I moved to glance behind the screens but Kukiko was being truthful. There was only the *tatami* matting on the floor. I opened the wall cupboard and saw the mattress and bedding rolled up neatly beneath the bronze *kimono* and a few ordinary clothes. There was nowhere else to look but I returned to the larger half of the divided room and turned over the cushions. There was no sign of the Chinese tape recorder.

"There is nothing," Kukiko said.

"You have already searched?"

She shrugged. "What is there to search."

I came back to the centre of the room and faced her.

"We seem to spend a lot of our time searching for the same people. Why are you looking for Naoka?"

She stopped being offended and played me at my own game.

"Why is David Chan looking for Naoka?"

"Because I am a private investigator. I am trying to find a man who has disappeared and this girl says that she was his friend. I hope that she can help me." I paused there and tried to coax her. "I am being honest with you. Isn't there some common ground where we can cooperate?"

She gazed at me steadily, pursing her lips.

"What do you know about this girl?" she asked at last.

"About as much as I know about Kukiko." I was bland and regretful. "She is a beautiful mystery."

I was too evasive. She frowned heavily.

"I am sorry. I do not think we have anything left to discuss. There is no common ground."

"Is Naoka our common enemy?"

She smiled bitterly. "If you cannot recognize your own enemies, then it is definitely time for you to say *sayonara* to Japan."

She moved past me and opened the door. As she passed through to the microscopic kitchen she glanced back over her shoulder and said very carefully in English,

"*Goodbye*, David Chan."

Then Toji filled the doorway again. He stood with his shoulders hunched and his hands lifted to the level of his swollen barrel chest. His fingers dangled like fat talons on huge pterodactyl claws. His hungry smile, like a twisted yawn in the obscene flesh folds of his face, invited me to follow.

I declined the invitation and stayed where I was. Over his humped shoulder

I saw Kukiko stroll out into the corridor and then she was gone. Toji waited another half minute, then his expression registered contempt and he relaxed. He growled something that was obviously an extreme Japanese insult and slammed the door hard in my face.

I stood for a moment in the empty apartment and then crossed over to the window. I lifted the curtain and a few seconds later saw them emerge on to the pavement below. They were Beauty and the Beast, Japanese style, walking incongruously together towards a black car parked at the kerb. I had noticed it on the way in but had paid it no attention. Now I memorized the number although I doubted it could serve any useful purpose. If the *Yakusa* had thousands of members then no doubt they also had hundreds of cars.

I watched them drive away and then completed the job of examining the apartment. I opened the cupboard doors in the kitchen, rifled through the pages of the few books I found and shook records from their sleeves. There was nothing.

I put one of the records on the turntable and sat down on a cushion to wait for Naoka to come home. After both sides of the record had played I chose another. After that had spun to an end I decided that I was out of luck. Naoka was obviously away for the whole evening.

★ ★ ★

I drove back to Kyoto thinking over my latest encounter with Kukiko and wondering what it all meant. I wished that Naoka had come home, for I felt certain that the interest of the *Yakusa* could hardly be beneficial to her health. My instinct told me she was in danger and should be warned, but there had been nothing I could do except leave a note with my telephone number at the Kyoto Tower Hotel. When she called I could fix up a definite time and place to meet her again.

I arrived back at my base still deep in thought, but abruptly I realized that I had a whole new set of problems on my plate. Half a dozen police vehicles and an ambulance were congregated outside the main entrance to the hotel with their lights flashing ominously. A small knot of spectators had gathered and were being held back by two policemen in navy blue uniforms and peaked caps.

My first response was a sudden fear for Sharon. I parked the car and hurried into the foyer. Two more armed policemen were on guard and they moved to turn me back. None of the English-speaking hotel staff seemed to be available at that moment, but the desk clerk recognized and identified me. The two policemen hesitated and then let me into the elevator. One of them accompanied me on the way up, his eyes black and watchful and his right hand hovering close to the revolver that was holstered at his hip.

When the elevator doors slid open I saw that the police activity was not concentrated around Sharon's room but around my own. That stopped me for a second but there was no time to rethink. My police escort indicated that I was free to carry on. Although whether I would have been free to turn back was another matter.

The door to my suite was wide open. Inside I recognized only two of the small army of visitors. Sharon Vale was sitting in a chair looking shocked and pale, and standing over her with his hands clasped behind his back and a very serious expression on his bespectacled face was Inspector Yamamoto. He was asking questions but he broke off when my escort addressed him respectfully from the doorway.

He turned and stared at me in astonishment.

"Mister Chan," he said slowly. "This is a surprise. I did not expect you to return."

"Why shouldn't I return? This is my room."

"Come, come, Mister Chan — do not waste my time with innocent games."

I took another step into the room and then I could see over his shoulder into the bedroom doorway which was also open. Naoka was sprawled on her back on the crumpled carpet with what looked like a multitude of vicious stab wounds in her chest.

"You didn't finish the job," Yamamoto said grimly. "When we found her she was still alive, and she spoke three words before she died. She said — *It was the Chinese.*"

I knew what was coming next but he said it anyway.

"David Chan, you must consider yourself under arrest, for the crime of murder."

11

THERE was a long silence, while everybody in the room remained motionless and stared at me with expressions of undisguised curiosity and speculation. There were half a dozen Japanese detectives who had been busy opening drawers, dusting for fingerprints and generally scratching their heads, but now they all regarded me as though I was some peculiar new species of murderer totally outside their previous police experience. Perhaps they expected someone with two monstrous heads, or wielding a bloodied dagger. Or perhaps they were simply and pleasantly surprised that I should stroll in uninvited to save them all so much routine legwork.

Nobody had yet moved to slap on the handcuffs so I took a step closer to the bedroom. It was a shambles with the bed-clothes littered over the floor. I looked down at Naoka again and saw that her skirt and panties were missing, no doubt they lay in shreds amongst the tangled sheets and blankets. A nice touch to add motive, just in case Yamamoto couldn't think of one for himself.

I felt sad and angry. I suspected that Naoka had double-crossed practically everyone she knew, but she hadn't deserved this. The stabbing had been unnecessarily savage, calculated to put the police in a grim and hostile mood.

I looked back to Yamamoto and got back to our expected dialogue.

"I didn't kill her."

"Do you expect us to believe that she would lie with her dying breath?"

"No. She didn't lie. It was the Chinese who killed her — but I am not the Chinese to whom she referred."

"But she is dead in your bedroom, and there are no other Chinese in this hotel."

"But there are other Chinese in

Japan. At the moment I believe they are again staying in Osaka, at the Osaka Royal Hotel."

Yamamoto's plump face was solemn. His eyes blinked behind his spectacles. "You talk in riddles, Mister Chan. I do not understand."

"The Chinese you must question are named Shang and Hu," I explained. "They are members of the Red Chinese trade delegation which has been touring your country. However, this particular pair know nothing about trade and economics. I am certain you will find that they are the security men, the secret police agents detailed to keep watch over the rest of their comrades."

Yamamoto blinked again. His face was aggrieved. "The Red Chinese trade delegation are Japan's honoured guests. It would be impossible for me to question any member of their party without absolute and irrefutable proof that they are some way involved in this crime. You have much more explaining to do, Mister Chan."

I could see that it was going to be a long uphill climb and so I began at the beginning, telling him of everything that had happened since we had last met. He listened carefully, and from time to time scratched gently at his bristled hair. At all the points he considered unbelievable he blinked. When I recounted how Shang and Hu had tried to kill me on top of Nantai his eyelids snapped up and down with increasing speed.

"This story is incredible," he interrupted at last. "If these two men tried to kill you, why have you waited to report the matter? You should have gone straight to the police at Nikko."

"As you have said it does sound incredible. And as you stated earlier these men are not ordinary visitors but honoured guests. I did not expect to be taken seriously until I learned the reasons behind their behaviour."

"And have you learned their reasons?"

"Not yet."

"So it is still incredible." He paused

deliberately. "But you have admitted that the dead girl is known to you!"

I nodded. "Her name is Naoka. She works as a secretary at the Koga car factory, in the office of the chairman, Mister Shinjira."

"So this is the girl you went to visit this evening," Sharon blurted abruptly. She had been sitting in dazed silence, her blue eyes fluttering helplessly from myself to Yamamoto. Now she had jerked awake, but at the moment it was not to my advantage.

Yamamoto's eyes glinted behind his spectacles. "Miss Vale has informed us that you left the hotel with the intention of seeking out this young woman. It would seem that you found her, and invited her back to this room."

"That is false conjecture."

"Then please account for the five hours you have been absent during this afternoon and evening."

I did as he asked. When I mentioned Kukiko and Toji he blinked almost wearily.

"Again you mention this beautiful girl *Yakusa*, whom you call Kukiko. Will she collaborate your story?"

"It would be optimistic to hope so. I don't know where to find her, and even if I did it is unlikely that she would wish to be associated with the police in any way."

"So you have no real alibi for the time you claim to have spent in the dead girl's apartment." Yamamoto spread his pudgy hands in a gesture of polite despair, and smiled very sadly as he spoke.

I decided not to argue the point. Even if he could find Kukiko, and by some miraculous chance she could be persuaded to speak up in my favour, there was still the time that I had spent waiting alone for Naoka's return that would be wide open to speculation. I had passed no one as I left the building, and as far as I knew no one had seen me leave. As my philosophical father — or perhaps it was my mother — had once said, there is no satisfaction in flogging a dead donkey.

"Even so," I told Yamamoto calmly, "You do not have any evidence that I killed this girl, only the circumstantial evidence that she was found in this room. Surely there are enough doubts and complications surrounding this case to warrant a thorough investigation before we leap to the nearest conclusion. Such an investigation must eventually reveal the truth."

"What complications? And what truth?" Yamamoto was acting difficult. "You must excuse me, Mister Chan. I am only a poor Japanese policeman. All I know is that you have come to Japan and consorted with known criminals of the *Yakusa*. And that now a girl has been found brutally murdered in your room — a girl who has accused you with her dying breath."

"You know the reasons for my visit to Japan," I said patiently. You know I am searching for a missing man, and that so far both the *Yakusa* and the Chinese have tried to kill me to prevent me from continuing my search. Those are the complications which must be explained before we can see the truth behind this murder."

"Ah, yes," Yamamoto sighed grimly. "It may interest you to know, Mister Chan, that so far I have been able to uncover no evidence whatever to indicate that the mysterious Mister Tony Fallon has ever existed outside the imaginations of yourself and Miss Vale."

I stared at him. He wasn't blinking now and his eyes were very bright behind his spectacles. He was waiting for a reaction and when he didn't get one he turned his head to stare equally directly at Sharon. She looked petrified and I saw that she was wearing her necklace of white beads. She was clutching them into a knot at her throat.

"This is nonsense," she faltered at last. "Of course Tony exists."

Yamamoto frowned. Then returned his attention to me. "On the first occasion we met you informed me that this American had stayed at the *Yushimaso Ryokan*. You also stated you had visited the *Yushimaso Ryokan* and talked to Mister Sato who is the manager of that place. Now I must tell you that I also have spoken to Mister Sato. He does not know the name Tony Fallon, and there has been no American guest at the *Yushimaso Ryokan* for the past six weeks. Mister Sato is also unable to remember your alleged visit, Mister Chan. It is all very strange, is it not?"

It was a surprise to say the least. I puzzled over it but there was only one answer.

"If Mister Sato has changed his story then he has either been bribed or frightened."

"But why? And by whom?"

I needed time to think and then answered slowly.

"I would guess the *Yakusa*. The Chinese can be as ruthless, as we know from the dead girl in the bedroom, but they would not have the same fact-finding resources here in Japan, nor the necessary image to induce terror into Mister Sato."

"We come back to the *Yakusa*." Yamamoto folded his arms and looked more like a short, fat little schoolmaster than a senior detective. "What is your connection with the Yakusa, Mister Chan?"

"Why don't you ask Shino?" I suggested gently.

He blinked angrily and I knew I had touched a raw nerve. He couldn't ask Shino because obviously he hadn't been able to find him. I wondered whether that was why he was so determined to believe in my guilt, because he thought I had tried to make him look a fool. However, there was a point here that was worth making.

"If Shino cannot be found, then he must have good reason to stay hidden."

"Men like Shino are always difficult to find." Yamamoto spoke with a

199

definite irritability in his tone. "It means nothing."

"But you know he is involved."

"I know the two of you were seen together, talking as friends. And that is all I know about your relationship with the *Yakusa*. The rest is just words from your mouth, which have no confirmation. The stories in which Shino and then the Chinese have tried to kill you may be as imaginary as Tony Fallon, the man whom nobody can find."

"Have you talked to Mister Shinjira," I suggested. "He can verify that Fallon did visit Koga cars."

"Mister Shinjira is a busy and important man," Yamamoto said shortly. "After talking to Mister Sato there did not appear to be any need to disturb him."

"You are now investigating a murder, Inspector. You have a duty to question anyone who may have relevant information." I spoke firmly but in the back of my mind there was a nagging voice of doubt. I suspected that Shinjira had called in the *Yakusa* in the first place. If that suspicion was correct then Shinjira was either controlling, or controlled by, the *Yakusa*. Either way, if the decision had been made to erase all memories of Tony Fallon, then Shinjira's memory would also have elapsed.

If Sato and Shinjira were prepared to lie then only Naoka was left among the witnesses who knew that Tony Fallon had visited Kyoto and Osaka — and Naoka was very dead. The thought caused me to wonder briefly whether I could be wrong in believing that Shang and Hu were her murderers. I looked at Yamamoto and asked bluntly.

"Who heard the dead girl's last words? To whom did she say *it was the Chinese*?"

"The words were addressed to this police officer and his colleague." Yamamoto half turned to indicate the two alert young men in uniform who had stationed themselves on either side of the door to the corridor. "They are the crew of the first police patrol car to answer the initial call to this hotel. They came directly to this room, accompanied by the hotel manager. All three persons heard those words before she died."

That was enough weight of ear witnesses. I came firmly back to square one and the conclusion that the killers could only be Shang and Hu.

"Who raised the alarm?" I asked.

"I did, David." Sharon looked wretched and her knuckles were as white as the beads wrapped around her fist. "I heard a noise in here and saw that you had left your door slightly open. I looked inside before I closed it — What I mean is I intended to close it. The sound must have been the girl trying to drag herself across the carpet. When I saw her I just ran away and screamed."

"It's alright," I said soothingly. I didn't want her to blame herself. "Someone had to make the discovery."

I glanced into the bedroom again.

Yamamoto watched my face. A police photographer had been taking pictures, the click and flash of his camera barely registering as we had talked. Now he had finished and was waiting patiently for any final instructions from Yamamoto.

"Have you noticed," I said carefully, "Although the bedclothes are scattered and the bedside table has been over-turned, nothing has actually been broken. The picture is one of a violent struggle, and yet it seems that there was no noise during the act, no screams, no thuds, no smash of breaking glass. Does that not strike you as odd?"

"Perhaps. But perhaps the girl had no chance to scream. Her killer could have had one hand on her throat."

"One of them held her arms behind her back, *and* had one hand closed over her mouth or throat," I corrected gently. "The other used the knife. Then the scene was staged. Note the drinking glass and the bedside lamp on the floor.

Both are intact. The impression of a sudden sexual struggle had to look real, but it had to be created in silence to give the killers time to escape."

"An interesting theory, Mister Chan. But I would rather hear your explanation for the strip of elastoplast that repairs your left hand."

"I cut myself during the chase on Mount Nantai."

"How, exactly?"

"I slipped and fell. I gashed my hand on a sharp stone."

"A sharp stone," he repeated sadly. There was no sarcasm in his voice, but his raised eyebrows invited everyone within hearing to share in his disbelief. "Are you sure that you did not injure your hand in a wrestling match over a knife?"

"I am positive."

"Mister Chan, I am not satisfied." Yamamoto spoke heavily and his face was stern. "I must confess that as yet I do not know exactly what happened in this room, or why. The only clear fact is that this young girl has been murdered. I need to make a thorough investigation into her background. And into your background and the background of Miss Vale. The circumstances in which you both come to be involved in this affair are, to say the least, very confusing. Especially do I need to make a thorough investigation into your contacts with the *Yakusa*."

He paused hopefully, as though at that moment I just might have broken down to confess. I had nothing to say and waited. He shrugged, a movement that added a few more wrinkles to his crumpled suit.

"So, Mister Chan, we must continue our conversations, but not here. These officers have their work to do and we are in the way. You must come with me to the Kyoto police station. There I will request your transfer to Osaka. I prefer, if possible, to have you on my own ground." He turned apologetically to Sharon. "Please, Miss Vale, you too must accompany us."

Sharon stood up reluctantly and asked for time to pick up her handbag and coat. Yamamoto sent one of his uniformed men with her and then conferred and issued orders to the detectives who were to remain behind. While we waited for Sharon to return I had a few seconds to indulge in some grim meditation.

Naoka's dying words meant that her killers had to be Shang and Hu, but it was equally obvious that Yamamoto was not going to offend his country's honoured guests with an enquiry based only on my suspect advice. The political storm that would blow up if he put a foot wrong in that direction would ruin his career, regardless of the harm it would also do to Japan's trade relations with China, so I could hardly blame him.

If, at the same time, the *Yakusa* were deliberately covering up all the links to Tony Fallon, then I was in a very awkward position indeed.

I had been in awkward positions

before, with the police in Hong Kong, but there the position was always less bleak. In Hong Kong I had good friends, a lawyer who would not hesitate to defend me, and I could always call upon the exceptional detective talents of Belinda and Tracey to carry on an enquiry while I was detained. Here I knew no one, except Ken Kenichi of whom I had professional doubts. I was on my own.

I had the cold feeling that once I saw the inside of a Japanese jail I would be very lucky to get out again.

Sharon returned and Yamamoto was ready to move. He picked up his hat and raincoat and invited us to procede him into the corridor. The patrol car officers in uniform had already moved outside. Sharon walked out slowly and I joined her.

"If your home ground is Osaka, then why are you handling this investigation in Kyoto?" I asked Yamamoto casually as he moved up behind us.

"Because of your *Yakusa* connections," he answered simply. "Technically this is a case for the Kyoto police, but police cooperation between departments is very good in Japan. Because you were involved, I was informed. There are formal courtesies to be observed, but I am confident that you can be transferred to Osaka for further conversations."

He meant interrogation but his was the more tactful word. We were approaching the elevator with the two uniformed men slightly in the lead, Yamamoto between myself and Sharon, and four plainclothes detectives, presumably from the Kyoto Criminal Investigation Department, trailing behind in a close bunch. When we stopped one of the uniformed men pressed the button for the elevator.

We waited in silence, my mind returning to its grim and fruitless meditations. There was a faint humming sound as the elevator car came up from the ground floor, and then a gentle thump as it stopped. The doors before us slid open.

For once the eternal Japanese politeness played into my favour. Both Yamamoto and the nearest of the uniformed men from the patrol car indicated to Sharon that she should step first into the elevator. I started to follow her and then spun on the ball of my right foot.

Maybe some of the men around me were karate experts, but I didn't practise karate and judo every day of the week for nothing. My right fist exploded under the uniformed man's jaw in the same second that my left foot kick smashed into his crew-mate's kidneys. As they went down my stiff-finger right jab scored in Yamamoto's fat stomach and he staggered back winded and gasping into the rest of the column. One tough young hero avoided his superior's flailing form with a neat side-step and challenged me at my own game. He came forward with a lightning fast throat chop and a kidney jab, either of which would have put me down among the bruised and battered if they had landed. I blocked the first and caught his wrist on the second, putting a vicious spin on it that hurled him against the corridor wall.

I stepped backwards into the elevator and stabbed the ground floor button.

One of the older men was on his knees and clawing out a gun from a shoulder holster. He had it levelled as the doors started to slide shut.

I took a long fast kick, my toe just reaching the tip of the gun barrel and spinning it out of his hand. Then I jerked my leg back a split second before it would have been crushed as the doors banged together.

Smoothly the elevator began to descend.

12

BEHIND us the third floor exploded with shouts and curses more ear-shattering than the massed fireworks of the annual New Year celebrations in Hong Kong. It made me glad that Sharon did not understand Japanese, for I had no doubt that there were a variety of choice obscenities raining down upon us that would have made her innocent cheeks blush crimson. Instead she was white and horrified, and I wondered if she had any doubts in her own mind on the subject of whether or not I had murdered Naoka.

The lift was rushing down fast and there was time for just one question,

"Are you coming with me, or staying behind?"

She hesitated for two seconds, but then a hint of the forced determination I had always suspected was there showed through the helpless, bewildered female facade.

"I'm coming with you," she said hoarsely but firmly.

The elevator stopped with a bump and I grabbed her hand. Before the doors were half open I had pushed through shoulder first and was streaking across the foyer like a greased greyhound, dragging Sharon at arm's length behind me.

I knew there had to be at least one policeman on duty, the man who had remained below when his companion had escorted me up to my room. He was moving in fast, alerted by the shouts from above. He had both hands at his right hip as he jerked his revolver out of his holster, but then I gave him a high flying kick in passing. Thai boxing is another of my oft-practised sports and when the sole of my shoe slammed under his breastbone he was bowled over backwards. He was just an open, gasping mouth in a startled face and then he was gone.

I crashed through the main doors and out on to the pavement. Ahead the way was blocked by the parked police vehicles. To the left was the waiting ambulance and on the right of the hotel forecourt the parked cars of the regular residents, including the red Datsun. However, two of the flock of waiting policemen had possessed the forethought to position themselves beside my car. They, and all the rest of the surrounding cowboys in peaked caps and navy-blue uniforms, were already performing the first clawing movement in the ritual dance of the hollywood gunfighter.

I didn't stop to see whether they could shoot as well as draw. I just dived left and put the big, solid ambulance in their line of fire as quickly as possible. The two ambulancemen jumped out of my way with more haste than dignity, for which I was truly grateful. I don't really enjoy hitting people whose intentions are all for the public good.

We ran desperately and we were in luck. One of the rattling streetcars that supplemented the Kyoto bus service had just left the front of the hotel and was turning up the main avenue alongside. I yanked Sharon across the tracks under its nose as the local constabulary scrambled past the intervening ambulance with guns drawn, and then the streetcar lurched between us to frustrate them again.

As the back of the streetcar drew level I locked my left arm around Sharon's waist and jumped for the footboard. My right hand locked on the door handle and we were carried away as the streetcar continued its clanking journey.

There were white, startled faces packed against the windows of the long carriage, so of course another uproar immediately began inside. I don't think any of them realized fully what was happening, for most of the bespectacled moon faces showed either anger at my stupidity or an embarrassing concern that I might break both our necks. The streetcar had started to pick up its full speed as it came out of the corner but now it began to slow again as the commotion warned the driver that something was wrong.

By this time we had been carried sixty or seventy yards, almost to the next road junction. I dropped off and ran on, still towing Sharon at high speed, and making sure that I stayed in front of the streetcar to block off any police bullets.

At the next turning I swung right. I now had the corner of a nice solid building between myself and the pursuing law, but it was too soon to linger. I kept going, dashed across the road between two startled motorists who honked their horns in a skidding frenzy, and then I was off up the next road to the left. I made three more twists and turns and by then Sharon was dragging and sobbing in my wake. I was also gasping a fair bit myself.

There were no thudding boots or flashing headlights immediately behind, but I knew it was only a matter of time. We had emerged beside the river where a line of cars were parked and I ran a criminal eye over the selection available. We needed transport and I settled on a small Mazda saloon that was both old and inconspicuous. It was locked but in my wallet I carried a small selection of lock-picking tools.

The one I chose was a simple screwdriver, bent at right angles one and a half inches from the blade. It pierced the rubber seal surrounding the quarterlight with no difficulty rind turned the catch inside in a matter of seconds. I reached through the quarterlight, unlocked the door on the inside and opened it. I pushed Sharon in and over to the passenger seat.

I flipped the bonnet up and it took me another twenty seconds to fix the wires and start the engine. I closed the bonnet, jumped in beside Sharon, depressed the clutch, shoved in second gear and we were away.

I was quite pleased with the speed of my performance and Sharon was duly impressed. When her bosom had stopped heaving and she could talk again she asked hoarsely,

"David, how and where did you learn to steal cars?"

I smiled at her. "Once upon a time in Hong Kong I worked on a case where a car thief was charged with murder. He was a very good car thief, but he was also a family man with a wife and six hungry children and murder wasn't his line. I was able to spotlight the real villain and the car thief was very grateful. He taught me a few of the basic tricks of his trade."

★ ★ ★

I got clear of Kyoto as quickly as possible, but I didn't take the obvious expressways to Tokyo or Osaka. I reasoned that if Yamamoto was smart enough to set up roadblocks then that was where they would be. Instead I followed the road signs west to Kameoka, which seemed to be the nearest direction to nowhere in particular.

We reached Kameoka in half an hour, despite the sluggish pace of the old Mazda which felt as though it needed a new set of pistons at least. The town was small, a few winking lights and bare streets emerging briefly from the night. A branch road turned south and I followed it. Sharon read the latest batch of road signs as they swung through the beam of our headlights.

"You're going back to Osaka?"

I nodded calmly. "That's where the answers are, Sharon. The Red Chinese trade delegation are still in Osaka. The *Yakusa* are based in Osaka, and so is the Koga car factory."

"But isn't this exactly what Yamamoto will expect?"

"Osaka is a very big city," I assured her. "Providing we can get there before this car is reported stolen there's a fair chance we can stay out of sight. Just twenty-four hours might be enough for me to turn this case upside down."

"But how, David? What can you do?"

"I'm thinking about it," I consoled her blandly.

She didn't find that at all satisfying, but she didn't ask again. She was still recovering from the shock and physical exertion of our flight and became locked in her own thoughts. It was a silence of mutual agreement, for there were things she didn't want to tell me, and things I was not yet prepared to tell her.

I remembered that earlier this morning she had expressed a positive determination to accompany me on my next trip, and wondered ironically if she was already having regrets.

* * *

Whoever owned the Mazda had left a battered suitcase on the back seat, it was full of sales literature and samples but it tempted me to accept the risk of booking into another hotel. Travellers without luggage were often suspect, and usually asked to pay in advance, but a suitcase was a badge of legitimacy.

We reached a small town called Ikeda, some ten miles short of Osaka but on the route from Osaka International Airport. There were several small hotels and I picked one with a dark adjoining lane where I could park the car out of sight. Sharon was by now looking very dubious, but at this stage there was nothing much that she could do except tag along. I took her arm politely, lifted the suitcase and marched boldly into the hotel.

It was all very easy. The hour was late, coming up to midnight, but being so close to the airport the staff were accustomed to departures and arrivals at odd hours. I booked us into a double room for two nights as Mr and Mrs Daniel Price, borrowing the name from a distant acquaintance in Hong Kong. Our nationality I gave as American with an address in the United States. The polite request for our passport I fended off by explaining that it was in the suitcase, we were tired after a long journey, and I would present it tomorrow after we had slept and unpacked. The man behind the reception desk hesitated for a few seconds, but then his intrinsic Japanese courtesy tilted the balance. Guests were often awkward but must never be offended. He bowed politely and assured me that he would be pleased to inspect my passport in the morning. Then he selected a key and escorted us to our room, manfully hauling our suitcase full of brochures, electric hair dryers, kettles and pop-up toasters, which he placed with due reverence just inside the door.

After he had gone Sharon stared in silence at the double bedding and mattress that had been made up on the floor. I removed a pillow and a blanket and dumped them on the *tatami* in the corner.

"The rest is all yours," I assured her.

She turned to me with a face that was still troubled.

"David, what happens tomorrow?"

"I shall leave early. I've got a lot to do. You'll be safe here, and if our friend mentions the passport again you can tell him that your inconsiderate husband has it in his pocket. Tell him I had to change some travellers cheques."

"But what will you be doing?"

"Sight-seeing in Osaka, temples mainly." I smiled briefly. "I hope to find the Grand Monk Morita."

"Won't that be dangerous?"

"If I'm successful, yes. That's why you're not coming."

★ ★ ★

I slept for six hours and then left quietly. Sharon was still asleep, sweet

222

as a child with her eyes closed and her blonde hair spread in loose, soft waves over the pillow, and I was careful not to wake her. She had not argued yet, but I was afraid that the uncertain determination that lurked beneath the surface might re-assert itself and she would insist on joining me.

I let myself out of the hotel and hurried round to the car, Ikeda was too small a place for a wanted vehicle to remain unnoticed and I had to get the old Mazda out of town before the local populace were awake and observant enough to read the number plate. Once on the road again I felt happier and relaxed behind the wheel.

I drove into Osaka and passed the Royal Hotel. The Red Chinese were spending their last few days there, winding up the final rounds of talks and bargaining with Japanese trade officials, and I knew I had forty-eight hours at the most in which to break this case open. However, I didn't dare stop at the Royal. Yamamoto would have the place crawling with cops. At this moment I knew I would stand more chance of penetrating the Imperial Palace in Tokyo and assassinating the Emperor than I would have of reaching Shang and Hu.

I drove on to the equally sumptuous Osaka Castle Hotel, parked the car and went inside. Curious stares from a half awake desk clerk and a sleepy doorman followed me to the public telephone booth, but they were a risk I had to take. I closed the glass door firmly behind me and dialled Ken Kenichi's home number in Tokyo.

The phone rang for half a minute before he answered, his voice yawning and resentful. I suspected that if he hadn't been a well-bred Japanese he wouldn't have answered at all.

"This is, David," I told him. "I apologize for breaking your sleep, but I have to know if you have any information yet on this man Robert Baxter?"

"I'm working on it," Kenichi said

slowly. "Yesterday I visited four motor car factories in the Tokyo area. Baxter has already called at three of them looking for Tony Fallon. The manager of the fourth factory promised to telephone me immediately if Baxter appeared there. So far he hasn't left any contact address, but I think it is only a matter of time before I find him."

"Try to speed it up, Ken. Finding Baxter has suddenly become urgent."

"I will try." His tone was cautious. "But what has necessitated this sudden urgency?"

"I can't explain over the telephone. But, Ken, please don't call me at the Kyoto Tower Hotel. Whatever you get, wait until I call you."

"I understand your instructions, David, but not your reasons."

"Forgive me," I begged him. "My behaviour is bad but I have no time. *Sayonara*."

"*Sayonara*," he repeated doubtfully.

I put down the telephone and

frowned. Then I picked it up again and dialled the international exchange. There was one advantage in making calls at six-thirty in the morning, they were put through very quickly. Two minutes passed and then I had a line to the apartment that Belinda Carrington and Tracey Ryan shared in the white block overlooking Hong Kong's Happy Valley race track.

"David," Belinda moaned irritably. "What an ungodly hour to get a girl out of bed. I'll bet you haven't even been to bed, you've just been wallowing in geisha girls and orgies all night — but we respectable girls have to get our sleep."

"Belinda, it's not like that — and I need that information from Detroit in a hurry."

"You're in trouble." Her well-modulated English voice was both positive and worried. "David, why is it that whenever Tracey and I let you out of our sight you immediately get yourself into some sort of a mess?"

"I'm accident prone," I admitted. "What have you got from Detroit?"

"Very little." She was wide awake now and gave it to me straight. "The man you wanted, Hank Miller, was listed in the directory, but it took me a couple of days to get hold of him. He was out of town on a case. We did talk on the telephone yesterday. He said that he'd never heard of anyone named Tony Fallon, and he'd never been approached by anyone named Sharon Vale. I gave him descriptions and the Detroit addresses that Sharon gave to us and he's promised to check them out. I'm expecting him to call back with anything he's got later today."

"Thanks, Belinda, I'll do the same."

"David, what's happening over there? What sort of trouble are you in?"

"Nothing I can't handle," I said with foolish bravado. "I'll tell you all about it when I get back to Hong Kong."

She wished me luck and I rang off. Neither call had brought any tangible results and I felt frustrated. I went back to the car and drove out to the dockside suburb of Kamagasaki.

Prowling around temples in search of the Grand Monk Morita might have been one way of renewing my contact with the *Yakusa*, but I doubted if I could short-cut my way direct to the top man. There was another alternative, but until I knew exactly what game Sharon was playing it seemed safer to tell her the occasional lie.

If there had been a choice I would have preferred to locate Kukiko, but I had no idea of where to start.

That left Shino. Yamamoto had told me that Shino spent part of his time as an organizer of labour in the Kamagasaki docks. He had to be well known in the area, so it was there I hoped to find him.

13

KAMAGASAKI was a grey and squalid suburb, like dockland anywhere. It was an area of grimy lodging houses which I would not have cared to penetrate too deeply. It was bounded by railway tracks and dock basins, and any sprig of cherry blossom that dared to grow here would soon have been strangled by dirt and soot. Its people were shabby, down-at-heel and shivering in the cold, misty air of morning. Most of them were men, the unemployed and the unemployable.

The activity I expected was not outside the dock gates where I would have assumed it to be. Instead it was outside the local labour exchange. There were rows of battered buses and vans pulled up in the street, and groups of men squatting and bargaining along the pavements. Their faces were unshaven, hollow-eyed and hungry. They milled like flocks of sour sheep searching for a shepherd.

Yamamoto had said that the *Yakusa* recruited day-to-day labour, which meant that recruitment had to take place every morning. A glance at the windscreen of each bus and van showed a placard with a scrawled price, mostly around three thousand yen, which meant that this was where it was all happening. Three thousand yen was just under nine US dollars, which I guessed was the daily rate for a hard day's slog in the docks.

I pulled over to the kerb and stopped. The street and the pavements were crowded but there wasn't a police uniform in sight. I got out of the car and slammed the door behind me. I couldn't lock it because I didn't own the keys, so I could only hope that it wouldn't be stolen again after I had walked away.

I approached the first group on the pavement. They were a dozen men in worn scarves and overcoats, and one smart young man in a suit with a white polo-neck shirt. They were all squatting and waving their hands in animated talk, but fell silent when I reached them. They stared up at me with curious faces and the young man got slowly and cautiously to his feet.

"I am looking for Shino," I told him quietly, knowing that he would only recognize the name. His face registered nothing, but I repeated the words before bowing politely. He returned the bow and I withdrew.

I walked past the next three groups which were close enough to have observed what had happened. At the fourth group I stopped and repeated the performance. I tried once more further down the street and then crossed over to try my luck on the opposite pavement.

In all I approached six of the neat young negotiators. They all wore the regulation dark suit with the white polo-neck shirt, and they all regarded me with steady eyes and blank faces. They were all under thirty, and they all reminded me of the man I hoped to meet.

When I was satisfied that the whole of Kamagasaki knew my purpose I went into a cheap but prominent restaurant and sat in a window seat with a cup of Japanese tea. I was certain that the news of my presence would reach Shino, and although the entire Osaka police force had failed to find him I had made sure that he could find me.

I waited for an hour. By then all the waiting vehicles had filled up and dispersed and the luckless ones who had found no work had begun to drift away. I drank three cups of the virtually tasteless, pale green tea and ate a basic breakfast of fried eggs and bread rolls. After that I began to wonder if I was wasting my time. It was possible that Shino would suspect some kind of a police trap and if so he would not come within a mile. Or, more simply, he may have considered it wise to take a long vacation somewhere far away from Osaka and all his old haunts.

I gave it another half hour while I tried to work out an alternative course of action. I needed an alliance with the *Yakusa* and it was beginning to seem that a long haul around the score of local temples in search of the Grand Monk was my only remaining hope. Then a large black car pulled up at the kerb outside the window where I sat, and I knew my luck was in. There were two men inside in the familiar double-breasted pin-stripe suits. Their unlovely faces looked as pugilistic and unfriendly as before, but at least they had turned up to renew our acquaintance.

I watched them walk across the pavement and enter the restaurant. They were my old friends, Tweedle-dumshi and Tweedledishi.

I didn't turn my head as they went up to the counter, nor when they returned to the empty table beside me with two cups of coffee. They drank the coffees noisily but without a word.

Then I sensed them staring at me.

I turned my head.

Our eyes met. I couldn't return both stares without going cross-eyed so I fixed on Tweedledishi. He remained silent. Finally he shrugged, a gesture that could have meant anything or nothing. The two of them got up and returned to their car.

I followed dutifully. Tweedledishi climbed in behind the wheel. Tweedledumshi got in the back seat and I slid in beside him. Tweedledishi started the car without turning his head, but Tweedledumshi at last gave me an evil, broken-toothed smile. He produced the close-fitting dark glasses I had seen before and obediently I put them on. I was blind again and the car moved away.

It was a thirty minute journey and they said nothing. They didn't speak English so any attempt at conversation would have been a waste of time.

When they stopped I was helped out of the car, steered over a narrow pavement and into an unseen building. There was a flight of wooden stairs to second storey level, and then a sixty paces walk. Judging by the bare floorboards and the lack of doors I deduced that we had to be in some kind of hall. There was a door, the sense of being in an enclosed corridor, and then another door. We stopped, and Tweedledumshi retrieved his special black painted glasses and dropped them into his pocket.

I was facing Shino. He wore judo clothing, loose white jacket and trousers with the brown belt of the first *Kyu* grade, one rank below the black belt of a master. I was entitled to wear the black so if he hoped to impress me he was mistaken. Behind him stood the inflated Japanese answer to the Hunchback of Notre Dame, Toji, similarly dressed but with a plain white belt.

Shino had his arms folded across his chest, a handsome pose. And he was smiling, his teeth very white and a bright glint in his slanted eyes.

"Mister Chan," he hissed softly. "I cannot decide whether or not you are a fool to seek me out in this manner. Do you really desire another ride on the New Tokaido Line?"

I smiled pleasantly. "I think we both realize now that the New Tokaido Line was a mistake. Kukiko will have told you that the Chinese tried to kill me on Mount Nantai, so you know I cannot be one of their agents. The Red Chinese are our common enemies, and we have a common interest in finding the American whom I believe they have kidnapped. I believe we can help each other."

"You signed a statement which enabled the Osaka police to issue a warrant for my arrest." His voice was still soft and he was still smiling, but his eyes flashed brighter. "That was not very helpful."

"I believed then that the *Yakusa* were just common gangsters," I said apologetically. "But since then I have talked with our mutual friend Kukiko and learned the truth. The *Yakusa* are the patriotic heart of the old Japan, the last of the *samurai* opposing the *zaibatsu* politics of the bad employers. Kukiko has shown me a new light."

Shino's face became empty of expression. He was no fool but he was curious.

"Why have you come, David Chan? What have you to ask, or offer?"

"An exchange," I said simply. "I have information which will be useful to you. And I believe that the *Yakusa* can obtain information which will be vital to me."

"How can we trust each other?"

I smiled sadly. "I must put my faith in the *Yakusa*. My side of the bargain must come first."

Shino stared at me for a full minute and then decided he had nothing to lose. "You may proceed," he invited.

"There is a girl named Naoka," I told him. "You may know of her, she worked as a secretary for Mister

Shinjira at the Koga car factory. This girl offered me her friendship, but she asked me many questions about my business in Japan. Later I found that she had recorded my answers on tape — with a machine which had been manufactured in Red China. The girl betrayed me to the Chinese. When I followed the trade delegation to Nikko the two security men with the group led me on to Mount Nantai and tried to kill me. They recognized my face because Naoka warned them of my interest and gave them my description. Because they failed to kill me they realized that Naoka had become a danger to them, and so they killed her."

I paused but no one interrupted. Even Toji and the two thugs who spoke no English listened politely. Shino's cold and handsome expression had not changed.

"They lured the girl to my hotel in Kyoto," I continued. "There they murdered her in my bedroom. They hoped I would be blamed and unable to trouble them any further, and they succeeded far better than they hoped. The girl was still alive when she was found and was able to say that it was the Chinese who killed her. She died before she could say any more. Because of this the police believe I must be the Chinese she accused."

Shino was amused. He smiled slowly.

"All of this is very entertaining, but how does it concern the *Yakusa*?"

"The *Yakusa* are concerned with finding Tony Fallon," I reminded him. "And if Naoka betrayed me to the Chinese after my visit to Koga cars — then it is logical to assume she also betrayed Fallon."

At last Shino was looking thoughtful. "What do you want?" he demanded.

"I want to clear my name of a murder charge. Tony Fallon is no longer important to me but he is important to the *Yakusa*. When we find him you can have him."

"How can we find him?"

"If he is not dead then the Chinese must hold him. This you already suspect or your would not have believed that I could be a Chinese spy, and Kukiko would not have been at Nikko. The two men responsible are named Shang and Hu. They kidnapped Fallon, with help from Naoka, during their first visit to Osaka. Their opportunities to move outside the planned programme for the trade delegation must be limited, so it should not be difficult to investigate such movements. The problem is that the police have refused to make any investigation because of the possible political consequences, and I cannot get within a mile of the Chinese because of the police guard."

Shino frowned. He had guessed what was coming next.

I scattered compliments to smooth the way. "The *Yakusa* have an influence equal to that of the police, perhaps even greater than the police. The *Yakusa* can succeed where the police bar the way and I must miserably fail. It cannot be impossible for the *Yakusa* to ask questions of the waiters and bedroom servants at the Osaka Royal Hotel. Perhaps some members of the hotel staff are already sworn members of the brotherhood of the *Yakusa*."

Two creases appeared in Shino's smooth forehead. He was thinking hard. He stared down at his folded arms. Finally he looked into my face again.

"I will take your proposal to the Grand Monk. He will decide. In the meantime you will remain here with my friends and Toji."

★ ★ ★

The waiting time proved to be long and tedious. The room was fourteen feet square with a few tall cupboards against the walls and the inevitable *tatami* matting on the floor. There was nothing else and I guessed that it had been chosen for its bareness. From outside I heard occasional thuds and muffled shouts of approval or scorn. I remembered Shino's judo clothes and guessed that I was being held in a side room to a sports hall.

I could have wished for more pleasant companions but the only faces I saw were those of my three guards. I nursed hopes that Kukiko might appear but they were all in vain. Tweedledishi and Tweedledumshi made occasional yawning conversation between themselves, but most of the time they just leaned with their backs against the wall. Toji offered a few animal grunts when the other two were being talkative but he soon became bored with all the inactivity. He went out, presumably to maul a punchbag or practise his scowl, or whatever *sumo* wrestlers do. From time to time he came back to glower through the door and assure himself that I hadn't eaten the other two.

I sat down with my back to a wall and practised meditation. After three hours had passed I began to hope that things were going my way, and that Morita had approved of his *Yakusa* minions playing detective to follow up the information I had given on Shang and Hu.

Another hour passed before I saw a fresh face. A young man in an athlete's track suit brought in three plates of food and three bottles of beer. Tweedledumshi and Tweedledishi sat on the floor to join me and we ate and drank in silence. The food was rice, crisp leaves of cabbage, a pork cutlet and a fried egg. There was a side dish of raw fish which I ate merely to be polite.

After the plates had been cleared away there was another four hours of boredom. I began to wonder how Sharon was faring and regretted the endless, bead-twisting anxiety I must be causing her. I felt that right now I would not have minded a few beads to twist for myself. I got up to stretch my stiff limbs and then sat down again.

My guards were accustomed to the performance and merely watched.

It was late afternoon, five o'clock by my wristwatch, when Shino at last returned. He was wearing his regulation black suit with the white polo-neck shirt and his smile was friendly.

I stood up to greet him.

"You were right, Mister Chan," he said with satisfaction. "We have questioned some members of the staff at the Osaka Royal Hotel, and we have learned that on their last visit the two men Shang and Hu did spend one night away from the hotel without the other members of the trade delegation. The man who cleaned their room remembers that on the following morning he found a half used book of matches beside the ashtray. The book of matches bore the name of an Osaka nightclub."

"Have you visited the nightclub?"

"I undertook the task personally. A waiter there remembers that the Chinese were the guests of a man who is a regular patron of the club, a certain Mister Fujimara."

"Then this man must be an agent for the Chinese. It isn't possible they could have staged the actual kidnapping of Fallon themselves. They must have arranged it through Fujimara!"

"That is difficult to believe. Mister Fujimara is well known and respected in Osaka. He is a very wealthy man. His home is on the island of Kamajima in the Inland Sea where he cultivates his own beds of cultured pearls."

Shino paused but then added, "However, like most Japanese businessmen his interests are varied. He deals in many other commodities and it is known that he exports to Red China."

"If he had some legitimate matter of trade to discuss then he would have talked with genuine members of the trade delegation, not with the security agents." I expressed a conviction that was suddenly very strong. "If Tony Fallon is alive, then we must look for him on this island in the Inland Sea!"

Shino nodded slowly. "Kamajima will receive a visit," he promised. "But I think that your usefulness is now over." He looked regretfully into my eyes. "I am sorry, Mister Chan, you have been most helpful, but you are too dangerous to remain alive."

Toji was behind him and he stood aside and gave an order. Obviously it was the order that Toji had longed to hear, for he advanced with a huge, evil smile. His monstrous hands were reaching out to break my neck.

14

TOJI was convinced that it was all going to be very easy, like pulling the heads off chrysanthemums or stealing rice biscuits from a baby. He had the physical strength to lift me up and break my spine over his knee, and probably he planned that for an encore after he had wrung my neck. He was a very happy neanderthal, with a yellow-toothed grin that would have looked good on a sabre-tooth tiger.

But first he had to get hold of me.

He broke into a lumbering charge and I caught his grasping right hand. I spun on my heel, my right shoulder slammed up under his armpit and I heaved. An ordinary man I would have thrown easily but he didn't have enough momentum behind his approach and he weighed twenty stone. He stumbled past me and his left shoulder hit me a glancing blow that would have been enough to sink the *Titanic*. I would have been knocked aside if he hadn't clawed me back into his embrace with his left hand as he hit the wall.

He was slow and he was clumsy, but he had a grip and he wasn't letting go. He roared in my ear like an insane mammoth as he twisted round and then he locked both arms around my waist. *Sumo* wrestling was normally a simple pushing and throwing match with no finesse, but Toji also knew how to crush an opponent in his hateful embrace. He had probably decided that he would break my back first and then my neck, and his good humour was restored as he brayed out the hoarse, cackling sound he substituted for laughter.

I could feel him bringing his knee up for leverage in the small of my back and knew I had only seconds before my spine snapped. My arms were free so I stabbed back savagely over my shoulders with stiffened thumbs. I was aiming at his eyes and I scored at least one direct hit. Toji screeched and released me in his agony.

I sprinted shamelessly for the far side of the room. When I looked back Toji was pawing at his left eye and jumping up and down in a frenzy of pain and fury. Tweedledumshi and Tweedledishi were keeping well back on one side of the room and Shino was watching from the other. So far they were making no move to interfere. I suspected that they were merely being wise, for Toji in a rage would hardly have the brains to distinguish friend from foe, and Toji in a blind rage would have killed his own mother.

He finally saw me out of the one squinted eye that was not streaming tears and let out another mammoth trumpeting that made even Shino flinch and cover his ears. Then he charged me for the second time with a face more hideous than the terrifying Gods of Wind and Thunder who had ruled over primitive Japan. And this time he had the full width of the room to get up speed.

I didn't have to try anything new or fancy. I just took one pace forward and went through the same routine. When I spun and heaved I put all my strength and skill behind it and he had enough momentum to keep going. He flew over my shoulder and his head smashed through the wooden panelling of the wall. His body was rolling as he ploughed forward, and he had half turned on to his back as the woodwork was flattened beneath his huge weight. There was another crack that had a different sound to the general splintering of timber and Toji screamed. He lay still in the great hole he had demolished through the wall and from the way his back was arched I knew that it was broken.

I looked away. The two thugs had open mouths and their thinking processes were frozen in a state of shock. Shino was also staring in utter disbelief but his reactions were faster. He must have realized that his brown belt grade wasn't enough, but one of the tall wall cupboards was right beside him and he yanked open the door. Inside it was full of sports equipment as I had suspected and he snatched up a six-foot *kendo* pole. He took an instant defensive stance, a training reflex, and then with a wild martial cry he sprang forward and attacked.

I did a somersault to the left and he missed me. The first swing of the *kendo* pole slashed into the broken woodwork above the mortally injured Toji. Shino wheeled fast and tried again but I heaved another of the tall wall cupboards into his path. As he dodged out of the way I reached the cupboard he had opened and grabbed a second pole to defend myself.

Shino crouched and smiled. *Kendo* fighting was a Japanese martial art and he was confident that I didn't know any of the tricks. He was right but I had no intention of fighting to the rules.

Shino attacked again and we exchanged a flurry of ringing blows. The *kendo* poles could be wielded like a two-handed sword, or used for thrusts and stabs like a spear. There was a third method of gripping the pole near the centre and raining blows with alternative ends like a demented paddler in a canoe. Shino used all three tactics, changing his grip with lightning fast moves to try and catch me unawares. I fought on the defensive and mercifully I was equally as fast on my feet.

Out of the corner of my eye I saw Tweedledumshi and Tweedledishi circling round the walls on either side. They were awake at last and trying to get behind me. Shino reverted to the sword grip and I did the same only just in time to deflect his slashing blow. As I did so I turned on the ball of my left foot and kicked in under his guard with my right. That wasn't in the rules of Thai boxing either because I kicked him square in the groin, but it was very effective. Shino reeled out of the fight for a few seconds and gave me time to deal with his friends.

Tweedledishi had pulled out his 8mm Nambu automatic, but while I had my back turned he wasn't sure whether he wanted to shoot me or hit me over the head. Before he could make up his mind I spun the *kendo* pole full circle and smacked down on his wrist. He gave a howl and the gun dropped and he stared white-faced at his limply dangling hand. Then he fainted away.

Tweedledumshi had started to jump but I rammed him in the middle with the blunt end of the pole and he folded up with another howl and lay gasping for breath on the *tatami.*

Shino whirled in for the third time with an expression of grim determination on his face. He tried every trick he knew in rapid succession and almost cut my legs from under me. Then he stepped on Tweedledishi's fallen automatic and stumbled. It was my first chance to attack and

I cracked him smartly across the knuckles. The *kendo* pole flew from his grasp and I clouted him hard across the head.

As he went down I threw aside my own pole, scooped up the Nambu automatic and ran.

I was only just in time. The sounds of battle had attracted attention and I could hear running feet in the corridor outside. A trio of young Japanese in shorts and vests were already bursting through the door and so I departed by the only other exit, the hole which Toji had unwittingly created into the next room.

I had to duck low and found myself in a room almost identical to the one I had left. There was a door on the far side and I dived towards it. I pulled it open and emerged into the corridor only yards ahead of the pack. They were surging up the corridor from my right and clamouring to get into the room where I had felled their champions. I was spotted as I made a fast turn left and they chased at my heels.

At the far end of the corridor there was a door to my right. I crashed through it and found myself in the long sports hall. The young Japanese in the track suit was coming at me on a collision course but he skidded to a stop when he saw the gun in my hand. I weaved past him and one of his friends made a grab at my arm. I swiped him across the jaw with the gun barrel and did an olympic sprint down the length of the hall.

They were in full cry when I reached the door at the far end, and I realized that it was odds against that I could outrun them all. I turned then and fired the Nambu, snapping two swift bullets low over their heads. They scattered in panic and I kicked through the door and dived down the flight of wooden stairs.

When I burst on to the pavement at ground level I found myself in the entrance to one of the arcade streets that lead into a maze of continuing arcades full of small shops. The main road lacked cover and I did not know how many of the irate young men behind me might also be armed once they had time to collect their weaponry, and so I turned into the arcade.

I continued running for the next five minutes, twisting and turning until I was satisfied that I had shaken off all pursuit. I put the gun away and slowed to a fast walk but all my senses stayed alert. When I emerged from the arcades and found another main road I walked along slowly until a taxi passed.

I waved it down and got inside.

"Osaka Castle Hotel," I told the driver carefully, and then settled back to relax.

★ ★ ★

We were several miles away and at this time of evening the rush hour traffic was hectic, which meant that I had plenty of time to think during the drive. I knew I was extremely fortunate to have escaped with my life, and now that I had learned all I needed to know through the *Yakusa* it was time to make another change of sides. I wasn't enjoying my role as the eternal deceiver, but on this particular case the alternatives were non-existent.

Right now I knew too much and the *Yakusa* wanted me dead. And I was reasonably certain that unless I got to Kamajima ahead of them then Tony Fallon would also end up dead.

Unfortunately I still didn't know enough and so I had to stop off to make another telephone call.

★ ★ ★

It was my third time lucky. I tossed a coin to decide whether I called the apartment or the office. The coin came down heads so I called the office. Belinda answered.

"It's good news day, David," she told

me cheerfully. "Tracey broke the drug-stealing case at the clinic this morning. The thief was caught red-handed and the police made the arrest. She's at the apartment now, so whichever number you called you would have got an answer."

"Good for Tracey," I said warmly. It was nice to know that my partners could still solve their cases even if I couldn't solve mine. I might end up in jail but at least the agency wouldn't go bust. "What about the report from Detroit?" I asked hopefully.

"Hank Miller called just before noon." Her voice took on a more serious note. "These long international telephone calls are costing us a fortune, David, but I think this one may have been worth it."

"Tell me," I pleaded. I wasn't usually impatient with my girls, but this was the second time I had taken the risk of telephoning from the Castle Hotel, and I had a horrible premonition that the police might burst into the foyer at any moment. At the right time I meant to give myself up, but the psychological advantage would be lost if I allowed them to catch me first.

Belinda sensed my urgency and came straight to the point.

"David, Tony Fallon does exist, and he was employed as an overseas buyer by Morrison and Brooks. What Sharon didn't tell us was that the firm sacked him six months ago for petty fraud. Fallon had been cheating blatantly on his expenses. Apparently he was a somewhat flashy personality who liked to gamble. He was heavily in debt." She paused. "He knew lots of girls but one thing he didn't have was a regular girl friend. He wasn't in the marriage market."

"So Sharon Vale doesn't have the relationship with Fallon that she claimed?"

"It doesn't look like it. Miller hasn't had time to check out the whole list of Fallon's dolly birds. And he wasn't sure how far we wanted him to press his investigation. But so far no one who fits Sharon's description has showed up in Tony Fallon's background. She definitely wasn't his fiancé."

That wasn't a surprise, but so far it wasn't much help.

"What about Fallon? Is he missing from home?"

"Yes. There's no evidence that he went to Japan, but he hasn't been seen around Detroit for the past four or five weeks."

"What else did Miller find out. It's important."

"It's coming, David. I'm not sure how it all fits together but I suspect that this could be what you need. Miller informs us that Tony Fallon was a close friend of a man named Richard Brett. And Richard Brett disappeared from Detroit at approximately the same time as Fallon. Isn't that curious?"

"Very. Who or what was Richard Brett?"

"He is — or was — " She didn't sound very certain. "An engineer working in the automobile industry. He was working on a design for a new car, but not with the conventional petrol-combustion engine. Brett was one of those engineers with a dream. He was working on the car of the future, the car that runs on an unlimited free energy supply, and doesn't add anything to the modern horrors of air pollution."

"It sounds like science fiction," I murmured sceptically.

"Don't be a cynic, David. There's a lot of work going on in this field, and even the experts admit that some kind of breakthrough is only a matter of time."

"And Richard Brett has broken through?"

"If he could be found, perhaps he could tell us. All I know is that he was working on two different aspects to the problem. One is batteries. Everyone knows that the electric car already exists. A number of experimental models have performed very nicely, but they have a limited range. To go any worthwhile distance all the available space has to be filled with heavy batteries, and that doesn't leave any room for luggage or passengers. The answer is to invent a new type of lightweight, miniature battery, and lots of very brainy people are trying very hard. They are using sodium sulphur, zinc-air, and special acid and fuel cells, but nobody has yet come up with anything that really works."

"Except possibly Richard Brett?"

"It does *seem* possible." Belinda had done her homework thoroughly as always but she was not willing to commit herself to something that was not yet proven.

"You said Brett was working on two different aspects," I reminded her. "What was the other?"

"Energy saving, coupled with a reduction of air pollution," she answered promptly. "You have to remember that even when miniaturized batteries do make electric cars feasible on a large scale, all those vehicles will still have to plug in to a power supply every few hundred miles. Instead of having millions of cars burning up petrol and fouling the air with exhaust fumes the world will have to build hundreds of extra power stations, all burning up the same amount of conventional energy and belching out their own smoke and pollution. The electrical car in itself is not the answer to the problem of providing continued mass transport."

"So it has to be solar energy," I guessed, because only sunlight was free and relatively unlimited.

"Right, David. You can go to the top of the class. There are already solar panels on the market made up of rows of silicone cells which absorb light energy and convert it directly into electricity. And there are experimental, dome-shaped buildings which draw all their heat and light from the sun. Getting back to automobiles, someone once tried mounting a large, flat tray on to the roof of a vehicle to catch the sun's rays, but whenever there was a strong gust of wind the whole thing flipped over sideways.

"Anyway, Brett stayed with the basic principles. Now that solar panels have been improved he believes they can be incorporated into the entire bodywork of the car, so that every square inch of surface area traps its due share of sunlight. If it works, and if he has solved the storage problem of holding large reserves of power in very small batteries, then he's designed an automobile that can go on for ever, with no fuel stops and probably a minimum of repair bills. Plus he's gone a long way toward solving the energy crisis and cutting down pollution."

"A highly commendable goal," I agreed. "But what proof is there that he's actually achieved it?"

"None. But it's food for thought, David. It might explain why Brett disappeared at the same time as Tony Fallon. And it might explain why Brett's car was fished out of Lake Michigan last week with bloodstains splattered all over the upholstery."

15

WHEN I emerged from the Castle Hotel there wasn't a policeman in sight. My luck was holding and I hailed a taxi and told the driver to take me back to Ikeda. He didn't recognize the name but fortunately he had a map of Osaka and its environs and that broke the language barrier. I was able to point out where I wanted to go.

I gave him an extra two thousand yen to make a fast trip.

When I walked into the hotel room in Ikeda I found Sharon in a state half way between panic and despair. She was on her knees, picking up the white beads from her necklace which had finally snapped from the constant twisting and tugging of her restless fingers. Some of the beads were stuck in the cracks in the *tatami* and she was having difficulty in getting them out. When she saw me she scrambled to her feet. Her blonde hair hung loose, her dignity was ruffled and her blue eyes flashed.

"David, where the hell have you been? The Japs have been pestering me all day for that Goddamned passport. And I've been worrying myself silly. You are supposed to be working for me, remember? I hired you to investigate this case — not to take me on the run from the cops and then dump me somewhere to go out of my tiny mind!"

"I apologize," I said gently. She wasn't the tame, shy little Sharon I remembered, but I had to concede that for her it had been a rough day.

"Why did you have to sneak out before I was awake? And what have you been doing all this time?"

If I was lucky I could get away with answering the last question only. "I was unavoidably detained by the *Yakusa*," I said hopefully.

"Then you found Morita?" Some of the sharpness went out of her tone and she stared directly into my eyes.

"No. I changed my mind. I didn't go looking for the Grand Monk. I decided it would be easier to find Shino."

She didn't look angry or disturbed, just faintly bewildered, and I realized that she hadn't despatched any thugs, Chinese, Japanese or otherwise, to hunt for me around the temples. The fear that she might have done so was just a nasty doubt in my own cunning mind.

I wondered briefly if Sharon Vale was her real name, and what kind of game she might be playing. But they were mysteries which would have to wait. If I challenged her now and spelled out everything I knew it would waste valuable time, and I still had no guarantee that any new explanation she might give would have any relation to the truth. Whatever else she might be, my client was a very accomplished little storyteller.

"How did you find Shino?" She asked in a voice that was faintly disbelieving.

"I'll tell you in the taxi. I've kept one waiting outside. We have to do some fast moving and some fast talking. If we don't then I have a hunch that a certain Mister Tony Fallon will be chopped up and fed to the fishes in the Inland Sea!"

* * *

We left the hotel three minutes later. There was more fuss and agitation over the missing passport but I paid for two nights and told them we were in a hurry. If they called the police at this stage it hardly mattered.

I gave the taxi-driver another two thousand yen in advance to make an equally fast return trip to Osaka.

On the way I told Sharon as much as I wanted her to know. I also took a calculated risk. The suit I was wearing wasn't cut to conceal a gun, so no matter where I stuck the Nambu automatic it made an obvious bulge. Ordinary honest citizens might assume that the bulge was nothing more sinister than a spectacle case or a tin of tobacco, but I knew I was about to place myself under the scrutiny of highly trained and extremely suspicious eyes.

I passed the gun to Sharon and said softly. "Keep that in your handbag. It just might be my ace in the hole."

She looked at it as though it might bite her, but then did as I asked, shoving it hurriedly out of sight.

A few minutes later we stopped outside Osaka Central Police Headquarters. I paid off a very happy taxi-driver with another generous tip and then carried our borrowed suitcase inside. Sharon walked uncertainly beside me. What her thoughts were I couldn't guess.

I stopped at the reception desk, gave my name to an English-speaking sergeant, and asked for Inspector Yamamoto.

* * *

He appeared promptly, looking surprised and curious. He didn't actually hurry into the reception hall, because that would have lost face, but he didn't dawdle either. His suit jacket hung open and his tie was loose, all the signs of a cop with a case that had developed into one long headache. His moon face smiled, but it was a polite mask for his inner confusion.

"Mister Chan, you never cease to amaze me. I expected several days to pass before you despaired of your position and gave yourself up."

"I am not in despair," I assured him. "But I wish to return this." I dumped the suitcase full of samples at his feet. "It is probably some little man's livelihood, so I don't want to retain it any longer than necessary. The car that goes with it you will find parked in the Kamagasaki area, in the street outside the labour exchange."

"Both the suitcase and a Mazda

saloon car have been reported stolen," Yamamoto said slowly. His eyes were fixed on my face and he hadn't yet made up his mind how to deal with me.

"I was responsible," I admitted. "I apologize. I must also apologize to you, Inspector, for the rudeness of my abrupt departure from the Kyoto Tower Hotel. I hope that neither you nor any of your officers were hurt?"

"Only dignities were damaged. And only face was lost." Yamamoto frowned at the memory and then continued grimly. "But police dignity, and police face, are important matters, Mister Chan. And assaulting police officers and escaping from official custody are very serious crimes."

"Kidnapping and murder are also very serious crimes," I returned blandly. "I know that a man has been kidnapped. And we both know that a girl has been murdered."

Yamamoto frowned again. A police car had drawn up outside to unload a couple of young Japanese who had obviously over-estimated their own capacity for *saki*. They were rolling unsteadily between two policemen and making a great deal of noise. Yamamoto's concentration was disturbed. He gave the new arrivals an irritable glance and then issued an invitation.

"Please come to my office, both of you. I think we have much to discuss and we can talk there in peace."

We followed his short, fat figure down a corridor and then up a flight of stairs to the second floor. Two solid young Japanese detectives trailed a few paces behind. We went into a medium sized office and found chairs. One of the young detectives politely assisted Sharon and then withdrew discreetly with his companion, just out of range of vision. I heard pages rustle and knew that if I turned my head I would see a pencil and notebook poised in his hand.

Yamamoto sat facing Sharon and myself with his hands resting on his fat knees. For once his eyes were unblinking behind his spectacles.

"Tell me," he began, "Why did you run away? And why have you returned?"

"It was necessary to run away because my investigations were not complete, and could not have been completed while in police custody. I have returned because I have uncovered new information to put before you."

"Please explain."

"First may I ask if you have made any enquiries about the two men I named, the Chinese, Shang and Hu?"

"That was not possible." Yamamoto spread his hands with more irritation. "The enquiries you suggest could have grave political and international repercussions. One does not lightly accuse honoured guests of murder, especially when they have diplomatic immunity and there is no proof!"

"That is unfortunate," I informed him calmly. "If you had asked questions you would have learned that Shang and

Hu did spend at least one evening without the rest of their comrades on the occasion of their first stay in Osaka. They visited a nightclub where they were entertained by a man named Fujimara, whom I understand is a dealer in pearls. He resides on an island called Kamajima."

"Mister Fujimara is well known in Osaka," Yamamoto said carefully. "It is the custom for Japanese businessmen to entertain lavishly in nightclubs or restaurants. Fujimara holds many large parties."

"This was a small, private party. And he did not invite ordinary trade officials — just the two secret police agents."

"How did you discover this?"

"A member of the staff at the Osaka Royal Hotel found a book of matches given away by the nightclub in Shang's room. A waiter at the nightclub remembers the meeting taking place."

"The name of this nightclub, please? And the names of your informants?"

"Those I cannot supply."

He blinked. "Then how can I verify this story?"

I smiled gently. "You could ask Shino."

That stirred him. He sat up and some of his politeness and patience began to evaporate. "Shino is no longer in Osaka!" He snapped.

"You are wrong, Inspector. Shino is making certain that the police cannot find him, but I made it possible for Shino to find me. Remember that neither you nor I were in a position to question the Chinese, or to check on their movements through the staff of their hotel. But the *Yakusa* have a wide influence and can draw upon a variety of loyalties. Shino was able to get the information I required."

Yamamoto stared at me angrily. Then he pushed his doubts away. "Where did you find Shino?" He demanded.

"His friends picked me up in Kamagasaki. They took me to a sports hall in the second storey of a building above an arcade street full of small shops. I made a deal with Shino. He kept it to a point by telling me about the meeting between Shang and Hu and Fujimara. Then he and his friends tried to kill me. This time I managed to fight my way out."

"This is the second time you claim to have escaped from the *Yakusa*," Yamamoto said sceptically.

"And once I have escaped from the police."

The reminder was painful. He winced, but he threw no further aspersions on my ability to play Houdini.

"What was the deal you made with the *Yakusa*?"

"One I had no intention of keeping, even if Shino had not broken his end of the bargain. I told them I was only interested in clearing myself of a murder charge — and they could have Tony Fallon."

"So we return to this man who never was," Yamamoto yawned wearily. "Today I talked to Mister Shinjira and he informed me that no one of that name has ever visited Koga cars. And he says he told the same to you!"

"Shinjira is a liar," I said bluntly.

Yamamoto looked hurt. "Shinjira, Fujimara, the Chinese! Mister Chan, it would be so much easier to believe you if you did not persist in accusing the most respectable of persons."

I learned forward earnestly. "Inspector Yamamoto, please believe this — Tony Fallon is not an invention, and if he is alive there is only one place he can be, the island of Kamajima. Shang and Hu tried to kill me on Mount Nantai, and they murdered the girl in my bedroom. The only possible explanation for those actions is that they are involved in the kidnapping of Tony Fallon. They could not have carried Fallon around on their prolonged tour, and so they must have an agent here is Osaka. That agent has to be Fujimara, because he is the only outside contact they have made."

"Fujimara is a very wealthy man. Why should he work for the Chinese?"

278

"All wealth has a beginning. It is possible the Chinese provided Fujimara's original wealth many years ago."

"Fujimara is an important businessman. I do not think you fully realize how important a businessman can be in Japan. And he has political contacts. Yet you make wild accusations and expect me to act upon them with no proof!"

"Shino seemed to believe that he had proof enough," I warned him quietly. "The *Yakusa* have their own reasons for wanting Tony Fallon, and unless we pay an immediate visit to Kamajima I fear your gangster friends will get there first."

That worried him, and I could see the twin horns of his dilemma. If he barged in on Fujimara on the strength of my word, and then found that I had been selling him a pack of half truths or lies, then he would create a political storm. If he sat back and did nothing while the *Yakusa* got away with a raid on Kamajima he would have unleashed a hurricane. Neither prospect was welcome.

"If you could give me the name of this nightclub?" he begged. "Something that I can check and verify."

"I can't and there isn't time. Shino may realize that my only course is to come straight to you. This is a race, Inspector, and we are already behind."

He gave up staring at me and looked at Sharon. She could only shrug sadly.

"I have to take his word too, Inspector. But I think David knows what he's doing."

"Very well." Yamamoto made his decision. "We will visit Kamajima and pay a call on Mister Fujimara. But we shall be polite and tactful. I shall pretend we have reasons to believe that gangsters may attempt to steal his pearls. All the questions must be left to me, but we shall all keep our eyes open."

★ ★ ★

A large black police car took us swiftly down to the docks where a sleek grey police launch had been summoned by radio. It was tied up loosely to a long jetty with its powerful engines still throbbing in a muted murmur. I noted the sharp bows and the searchlight mounted forward above the cabin. The night wind blew cool along the waterfront and Sharon shivered as we got out of the car.

Five of us went aboard the launch, myself, Sharon, Yamamoto and his two detectives. The craft had a three-man crew in navy blue uniforms, peaked caps, and polished black belts and holsters. I would have preferred a larger party, but Yamamoto had insisted that an approach in force was not yet justified.

Yamamoto spent a minute conferring with the crew and then the mooring lines were cast off. The launch headed out into Osaka bay and over the oily black waters we watched the pools of yellow light around the ships along the wharves. Unloading continued at all hours of the day and night, taking no notice of the darkness and the thin cold rain that was beginning to fall.

Sharon accepted an invitation to shelter in the cabin with the two detectives, but I chose to remain on deck with Yamamoto. I watched the freighters and the long sheds disappear into the yellow-blurred murk, and then the lights went out behind the curtain of rain.

Ahead the sea was black and choppy. The clouds hung low to hide the stars.

"Kamajima is half an hour," Yamamoto informed me. "It is a small island just offshore of Awaji Island, the large island that separates Osaka Bay from the rest of the Inland Sea."

Twenty minutes later our pilot called Yamamoto up to the wheelhouse. I followed uninvited and looked over the little fat man's shoulder.

On the small radar screen there was a tiny blip showing dead ahead, and racing us to Kamajima.

It was another launch, about the same size and speed as our own, and I knew instinctively that it was loaded with Shino and his trigger-happy gangsters of the *Yakusa*.

16

YAMAMOTO gave a terse order to increase speed and the launch strained forward as the pilot opened the throttles. Like a hunting shark it forged ahead. I felt the deck boards vibrate beneath my feet and behind us the white wake thrashed and foamed with increased violence. The sea rushed past swiftly on either side. The pilot divided his attention between the black waves ahead and the blip on the green glow of his radar screen.

Yamamoto looked anxious. He wasn't yet certain as I was but the presence of the launch ahead had him bothered. He fretted impatiently, but although we were closing the gap he knew there simply wasn't time to overhaul the mystery vessel and identify the occupants before we reached Kamajima.

Once his hand strayed towards the radio-telephone, but then he changed his mind and drew back. He was undecided and I knew he wasn't going to commit himself to calling up reinforcements yet.

I felt frustration, but there was nothing I could do. Until he knew that he could trust me it would be pointless to offer him advice.

The rain had stopped. Suddenly the clouds broke and a handful of pale stars glimmered through the ragged hole in the great, sulking canopy of darkness. Simultaneously we saw the white wake of the *Yakusa* launch, and the low black outline of Kamajima.

There were lights on the island, which I assumed to be the windows of Fujimara's mansion. Yamamoto had described the place so I was able to pick out or guess at the night-masked details as we approached. Dead ahead, acting as a beacon for both launches, was the splendidly ornate residence which Fujimara had built for himself and modelled on the villas of the old *Shoguns*. I knew it was situated above a strip of sandy beach. To the left would be long rows of sorting and packing sheds, with behind them the accommodation for the pearl workers. While to the right was virtually a small park of ornamental Japanese gardens.

All along the foreshore, except for the strip of beach immediately in front of the house, were moored long floating rafts of bamboo. On the underside of each raft dangled thousands of oysters, each one treated with the insertion of a minute spec of grit. The sensitive mollusc protected itself from irritation by covering the foreign body with thin layers of smooth white calcium carbonate, and thus a pearl was born.

It was an interesting process and I guessed that in daylight Kamajima would be a fascinating and beautiful place to visit. By night, and in the present circumstances, it was merely sinister, a silent, shrouded land mass threatening danger and violence.

The *Yakusa* launch was three hundred yards ahead without lights, her position marked only by the blip on the radar and the disturbance of her wake. She was making full speed now and the police launch could only keep pace. One of the police crew was poised to switch on our searchlight but he waited for the order. Yamamoto was struggling to focus a pair of night glasses but without success. We were now bouncing high on the waves.

I saw faintly the long, pointing arm of a small jetty, but the *Yakusa* launch ignored it and ran straight up to the beach. It grounded in shallow water and although I couldn't see exactly what was happening I knew that the men on board had scrambled over the side and were rushing to invade the island.

Yamamoto barked an order and our searchlight snapped on. A powerful beam of white light lanced forward to show up the *Yakusa* launch. The vessel had ground broadside on and whoever had remained at the wheel was struggling to bring her back into deeper water. The main landing party were splashing through thigh-deep waves toward the strip of yellow sand. I estimated a dozen men, and in the lead was a slim, determined figure whom I knew was Shino.

They didn't look back and panic when the light hit them. They were already in trouble and the spotlight seemed to be the least of their worries. They were hopping up and down in the shallow water and screeching with pain and anger. It was mysterious and bewildering sight. They looked as though they had run straight into a nest of crocodiles or a shoal of man-eating piranha, although I knew that neither menace existed in the Inland Sea.

Simultaneously two more brilliant white lights flashed into being. They were mounted high up on the beach and the twin beams merged with our own in a blinding dazzle that was fixed on the struggling men in the sea. The sound of guns spat angry bullets into the night and I sensed rather than saw the rush of men behind the lights who had hurried up to defend their island.

Two of the attacking *Yakusa* screamed and disappeared beneath the waves. I didn't know if they had been shot or if something in the sea had dragged them down, but I was sure that one of them was my old friend Tweedledumshi. The others made an effort to fight back, firing their handguns and making continued painful progress to the shore.

Shino reached the beach and knelt. His gun cracked and one of the spotlights near the mansion was knocked out in a smash of breaking glass. Due to all the shrieks and confusion I don't think that he was even aware that there was a third searchlight coming up fast behind him.

"Make for the jetty!" I yelled at Yamamoto. "Or the rafts. If we try to wade up to the beach we're going to walk straight in to whatever it is that has crippled the *Yakusa*."

Yamamoto was already giving orders, but whether he was translating what I had said I didn't know. His two detectives came out of the cabin with guns in their hands and reminded me of the Nambu automatic in Sharon's handbag. She appeared behind them, white-faced and uncertain, but she had left the handbag on the seat at the far end of the cabin. With the two Japanese blocking the cabin doorway I couldn't reach it.

Yamamoto reached for the radio-telephone and at last began gabbling his belated request for armed assistance.

Our pilot cut the throttles back as the police launch roared in. In their excitement one of the detectives blundered against his shoulder and for a split second our bows were knifing toward a head on collision with the first of the floating oyster rafts. The pilot flung the wheel over and we came round broadside with our hull scraping the bamboo. I didn't wait for the launch to manoeuvre round the jutting corner of the raft to the jetty but vaulted over the gunwale on to the raft itself.

I heard angry, startled shouts behind me but I didn't stop to explain. I knew that dead men tell no tales and so I had to find Tony Fallon as quickly as possible. I sprinted across the heaving surfaces of bamboo, jumping from raft to raft, and careless of the fact that there was probably a fortune in unharvested pearls beneath my running feet.

Some of the bamboo was very slippery, smooth and wet and in places fronds of seaweed had grown up through the lashed poles to create additional hazards. I floundered a couple of times and then reached the more solid structure of the jetty. I bounded up and dashed along the wooden boards to the shore.

The pilot of the *Yakusa* launch had succeeded in getting the craft out of the shallows and had turned against the side of the jetty with the bows pointing back to the open sea. Shino and his friends were not yet abandoned even though the odds were against them getting back on board. The slender figure of the pilot scrambled on to the jetty with a rope to make the launch temporarily secure. Only then did she hear the rapid pounding of my approaching footsteps.

It was Kukiko again. She dropped the rope and straightened up with the 0.32 automatic in her hand. For the third time it was aimed straight at my heart, and then she recognized me and for the third time she held her fire.

I skidded to a stop, raising my hands to shoulder level. I had just enough breath for a warning.

"Don't shoot, Kukiko. This time the police are right behind me. They'll arrest you for murder and that will be the end."

She hesitated, and I knew her actions would be influenced more by her loyalty to her friends than to any call for vengeance or friendship she might feel toward me.

"You can't help them," I insisted.

"But I owe you my life and I'll try to help you. Give me the gun and hand yourself over to the police."

She was helpless as a reed in the night wind, shooting frantic glances in both directions along the jetty. On shore Shino and his surviving companions were still waging a desperate gun battle with the hidden defenders behind the one remaining light. At the seaward end Yamamoto and his policemen were approaching fast.

I held out my hand.

"The gun, Kukiko, please."

She stared into my eyes. Her expression was unreadable except for the anguish she was feeling. I thought for a second she was going to shoot, but then she slowly lowered the gun. She didn't place it in my hand but just allowed it to drop limply at her side.

I left her to Yamamoto and ran on. There simply wasn't time to disentangle her fingers from the gun.

The war on the beachhead was almost over. Four of the *Yakusa* law sprawled on the yellow sand and the others were scattering to retreat behind the long sorting sheds with their wounded. They hadn't a hope but one man was still trying to reach the house and that was Shino. He was wriggling forward on his elbow and belly and firing as he went.

The defenders were getting sufficiently brave to emerge from behind the dazzle of their light. Most of them were vague crouched figures in the gloom but I recognized the tall figure of Shang and the slightly hunched bulk of his comrade Hu. I believe it was Hu's bullet which finished Shino, for the young *Yakusa* leader suddenly rolled over and lay still. His head had kicked back briefly as though taking a violent impact.

By this time everyone on the beach had realized that the police had arrived. The searchlight on the police launch was still raking its beam over the scene, and Yamamoto and his men were shouting the Japanese equivalents of "*Everybody stand still!*" and "*This is a police raid!*"

However, no one was standing still. The beach was clearing fast on all sides. As I arrived the main group of defenders, presumably the Japanese hirelings of Mister Fujimara, were retreating in good order toward the house. The *Yakusa* remnants had chosen the sorting sheds as a refuge, and I saw Shang and Hu slip away on the opposite side of the beach into the dark shadows of the park-like gardens.

I was surprised to find Shang and Hu on Kamajima, but their presence was an unexpected bonus which gave me a grim sense of satisfaction. I realized that tonight would have been their last night in Osaka, and consequently tonight offered their last opportunity to consult or make any final arrangements with Fujimara. The fact that they were here made Tony Fallon of secondary importance, especially as it was possible that he was already dead. If I could catch and confront either of the Chinese with the doubting Inspector Yamamoto then I would have proved my case.

I also remembered how brutally Naoka had been murdered, and despite her sins our love-making had been a sweet and enjoyable experience. I owed her something for that.

I decided I had sufficient reasons and justification to ignore everything else and concentrate all my energies on the Chinese.

I plunged into the gardens at full speed, but quickly slowed to a stop. I was surrounded by small pines, cherry and plum trees and a few tall cedars. There was a profusion of smaller shrubs and bushes I couldn't name and in the centre of the gardens I could see the slanted grey roof of a small shrine. The stars threw shadows and a dim light and the air was scented with the smell of mixed blossoms, plum, cherry and apricots, all sweetened by the recent rain.

There was still noise and shouting on the beach behind me, but there was no sound that could lead me to Shang and Hu here in the garden. I knew it would be vital to them to make themselves vanish and I guessed they would try to hide on the island until the police had gone. They had gone to earth somewhere but the faint prickling of the tiny hairs on the back of my neck warned me that they were close. Some positive instinct told me they had separated, and if they were aware that I had pursued them this far then it was questionable who was stalking whom.

I wished now that I held the Japanese Nambu which still reposed in Sharon's handbag. Or that I had delayed to wrestle Kukiko for her little toy. Even the paltry 0.32 calibre would be better than nothing.

I moved cautiously, not knowing whether I wanted to pray for more starlight or less. I placed each step as softly and silently as a feather in a breath of breeze as I eased my way along the shadowed path. The shrine appeared more clearly and I saw that the pillars and verandah railings were lacquered a bright vermilion. The beam ends under the eaves were carved into dragon's heads and painted black and gold. It was a Shinto shrine, dedicated to the old Gods of nature, and close by was a small lake spanned by a narrow, ornamental bridge which was also painted a vivid red. Irises fringed the lake and water lilies floated on the surface. Close by were a few stone spirit houses where the spirits of the dead were supposed to rest on their journeys back to earth. They looked like empty stone lanterns set upon waist-high stone pillars.

I felt that the spirits of the dead were very close. They were waiting for some new company.

I wondered if one or both of my enemies could be inside the shrine. My mouth was dry and my stomach was hollow, and the adrenalin was surging in my veins.

There was a movement from behind

the shrine. Hu stepped out into the open with his automatic levelled in both hands. The starlight gleamed on his teeth where his lips had peeled back in an animal snarl, and on the bulbous snout of the silencer he had screwed on to the barrel of the gun. Obviously he didn't want to attract Yamamoto and his policemen into the garden. He fired and the bullet spat softly towards me.

I was already spinning to my left, pivoting like a man who had been hit. The bullet missed me but I let out a strangled cry as I crashed sideways. My body flattened a previously tidy section of the shrubbery and my right fist closed over a handful of soil and small stones.

I froze.

I sensed Hu moving cautiously towards me, to check his kill and if necessary to fire the finishing shot. I heard his shoe crush another shrub near my feet and then I twisted back into life and hurled the handful of dirt into his eyes.

I had rolled as I moved and Hu's second shot smacked down into the earth where my head had been. He staggered back blinded with one hand clawing instinctively at his eyes and that gave me the second I needed to get to my feet. I shoulder-charged him and clamped both hands on his gun wrist at the same time. I twisted and he released the gun as we went down together, my shoulder slamming his chest and crushing the wind out of him.

We fought in silence as he had been trained to do. He tried to get a death grip on my throat but failed and we rolled apart. We both regained our feet and I let him come to me. Perhaps the fact that he still couldn't see properly impaired his judgement for he simply rushed me with no finesse. I threw him beautifully over my right shoulder.

It was unintentional but behind me was one of the stone spirit houses. Hu hit it headfirst at full momentum and two things happened. The stone spirit house was knocked off its pedestal and Hu's head caved in like a broken egg.

I didn't have time to hunt for the gun he had dropped. I was too exposed and I simply melted into the nearest patch of black shadow. Again I froze. My life was at stake in this game and I was relying on instinct alone. There was no time to think, dissect or analyze. When instinct said duck I ducked.

I waited for two minutes in the pitch darkness. Two minutes that were an eternity of sweat and tension. Two endless, agonizing minutes when it seemed as though time itself had stopped, terrified by the icy presence of some vast primitive and universal god of fear. The stars had stopped wheeling. The galaxies no longer revolved.

Then a shadow stirred from the gloom.

"Hu?" Shang murmured softly. And I realized that as yet he did not know whether his friend had won or lost.

Like a compulsive gambler I chanced

it all on a show of bluff. The dice of fate were rolling in my favour tonight, and although Shang had a silenced automatic levelled cautiously in his right fist, the psychological advantage was mine.

"Over here," I said in the same soft tone.

I used the Peking dialect and although my voice was hoarse I knew that Hu would have been equally breathless if he had won our fight. I straightened up from the black shadow of the shrubbery and stepped calmly into the starlight.

For a hair's-breadth of time Shang was fooled, and when he realized that my silhouette did not match up to the bulkier shape of his friend it was too late. I kicked the gun out of his hand.

He recoiled with a curse of pain but he came back fast. I gave him a stiff-finger jab to the belly and aimed another at his throat. He twisted away and as he turned he slashed backward and upward with the edge of his hand. The chop would have crushed my larynx if I had not side-stepped smartly. He wheeled full circle and lashed out with his foot. His heel caught my hip and sent me staggering. He closed in again and kept me on the defensive with a series of savage, lightning-fast jabs, kicks and chops.

Shang was a killer and his masters in Peking had trained him well. He knew every karate death blow in the book and he tried them all. I made sure that none of them landed on target but it was desperate work. We reeled through the trees and over flower beds in our grim, martial dance, and the sweet pine smell from the broken branches and the scent of crushed petals filled the air. Shang stumbled and I broke through his guard with a blow that smashed his nose. The blood gushed like a spray of red cherry blossom over his face and shirtfront.

His ice-cold composure snapped and he shrieked aloud. He exploded into fury and I had to fall back. We were on the edge of the small lake and the only way to retreat was on to the red-lacquered bridge. A rotten board gave way under my heel and for a second I was thrown off balance. Shang scored with a karate kick to the heart that sent me crashing down on to my back. He gave a high pitched scream and leaped into the air above me. He intended to land on my chest with his knees smashing in my ribs like two rows of brittle matchsticks but I rolled to my right. One knee hit my shoulder and the other crashed down on to the bridge. The whole structure collapsed beneath us and we were thrown into the shallow water of the lake.

It was bitterly cold and I scrambled quickly to my feet. My left shoulder felt as though it must be broken. Shang had the same problem with his right leg, and I learned later that he had shattered his kneecap. He struggled up more slowly with a tangle of water lilies in his hair and I hit him with a straight right fist to the jaw. His head snapped up and round and I hit him again with a karate chop. He fell with a broken neck and slid under the waist-deep water of the lake.

For a few moments it was as much as I could do to remain upright. I stared at the large round leaves of the water lilies that had draped Shang's head, now floating serenely where they belonged. I knew then that the tall Chinese was not going to surface again. He was dead and it was over, and remembering Naoka I had no regrets.

I moved my left arm until I had reassured myself it was not going to fall off. The shoulder hurt badly and I guessed that it would be one giant black bruise within the next few hours, but at least there were no broken bones.

I turned away and waded back to the shore. The little Shinto shrine was quiet and peaceful in the starlight, and only the scent of the crushed blossoms remained. I hoped that the spirits of the dead had found enough new companions, and that now they could go home.

I walked slowly up to the house, hoping that now I could wind it all up without any further action or excitement. For one night I had had enough.

But I was out of luck.

I ran straight into a man I had never met, but whom I recognized immediately. I had been hunting for him for a long time and his image was imprinted firmly in my mind.

Tony Fallon had his hands tied behind his back, and he was being urged forward by a plump, well-groomed but visibly sweating Japanese in a white dinner jacket. I assumed that the Japanese could only be the much respected Mister Fujimara, and in Fujimara's trembling hand there was another gun.

17

THE slanted roofs of the great mansion house gleamed silver grey in the starlight. The general silhouette suggested a magnified reconstruction of the golden pavilion in Kyoto and the whole edifice must have cost many millions of yen. Inside lights blazed and I could hear running feet and shouting voices. The police were at the front door, but Fujimara had obviously hoped to avoid them by slipping quietly out of the side exit into the gardens.

When he saw me he stopped dead and his face drained of colour. He had his left hand on Fallon's shoulder but suddenly he needed it there for support instead of restraint or guidance. His mouth opened and moved, but whether to threaten or plead it was impossible to say. No words came out. The events of the night had left him petrified.

I also stood very still. Fujimara was not another trained killer from the same breed as Shang and Hu. But a man who was scared sick with a loaded gun in his hand could be equally as lethal.

Softly, softly, catchee monkey. The old maxim flitted through my mind and I knew I had to play this game with care. The seconds ticked by and I spared a few of them to glance at Fallon.

Sharon's description of him had been accurate: five foot eight inches tall, husky build, fair hair and grey eyes. Well groomed he would have charmed the ladies, but right now he looked haggard. I guessed that he had had a tough time over the past fifteen days, and quite a few sleepless nights. He stared at me and swallowed hard. He was scared too. With Fujimara's gun in his back he didn't know how long he had to live.

"It's too late," I told Fujimara gently.

"Even if you do kill your prisoner, and then me, there is no escape. There's no time to hide the bodies and nowhere to run. If you use the gun you can only make matters worse."

He stared at me with the eyes of a trapped animal. His face was now as white as his dinner jacket and two streams of sweat trickled down from his temples and over his plump cheeks. He had lived the soft life and now he was well out of his depth. I guessed that he was clever, greedy and unscrupulous, but he was definitely not a man of violence. The harsh realities of judgement day had left him in a state of shock.

There was silent movement in the doorway of the house.

"Put down the gun." I had to speak more loudly to make sure the words carried past him. "It would be a mistake to kill Fallon now. A dead prisoner will be just as incriminating as a live one."

"No," Fujimara croaked at last. His

voice was thick with fear. He moved the gun to aim at my chest and added. "You must move out of my way."

"It is hopeless. The police will search all of this island. Your career as an undercover agent for the Chinese is finished."

I was talking only to distract his attention. Yamamoto moved up beside him like a hobgoblin in the gloom. The cold steel barrel of a police revolver pressed again the nape of Fujimara's neck and the inspector's free hand reached over the shoulder of the white dinner jacket to take the gun.

Fujimara collapsed.

★ ★ ★

We moved into the house, dragging the owner and dumping him without ceremony against the wall. Then Yamamoto produced a penknife to cut the ropes that lashed Fallon's hands behind his back. The American was grateful and began to massage his inflamed wrists. Yamamoto watched him for a few seconds but then decided that the man he wanted to question first was me.

"It would seem that I owe you an abundance of apologies," he said ruefully. "I saw the two Chinese on the beach. You followed them into the gardens. What happened?"

"They are still in the gardens, one in the lake, the other by the shrine. They won't be going anywhere."

Yamamoto blinked. "You killed them?"

"They were very dangerous men. And merciless. I had to fight by their rules."

Yamamoto frowned heavily, thinking of the political consequences, but then he cheered up. "Perhaps it is better this way. Alive they would be even more embarrassing."

I nodded bland agreement and then asked, "What happened to the *Yakusa*?"

"They have surrendered, together

with Fujimara's men who defended the house. Fortunately both parties had spent most of their ammunition and their energies in fighting each other. My men are thinly spread but they have everything under control, and reinforcements are on the way." He paused. "Our mutual friend Shino was amongst the dead."

I had no regrets, but one thing still puzzled me. "What happened when they hit the beach? It looked as though something attacked them in the shallow water."

Yamamoto shook his head. "It was nothing like that. I would imagine Mister Fujimara must have visualized the possibility of some kind of night attack by swimmers. The whole of the seabed in front of the house is scattered with dead oyster shells. The edges of these shells are razor sharp. Shino and his men simply cut their feet to ribbons before they reached the shore."

I looked down at Fujimara with new loathing. He had no backbone of his own, but he had made up for it with hired help and nasty ideas.

However, Yamamoto was now more interested in Fallon. He turned to the American with a slight bow and addressed him politely.

"You must be the man for whom Mister Chan has been searching, the elusive figure around whom this whole case revolves. I saw that you were a prisoner, but now I am curious to hear your full story."

"It's an easy one to tell," Fallon said slowly. He had been given time to think and he was prepared to bluff his way out. "These people kidnapped me. I had a date with a girl and something was slipped into my drink. Some kind of dope. When I woke up I was in this place — wherever it might be. They've been holding me here for over two weeks." He paused. "I guess they were trying to arrange some kind of ransom. Maybe they thought my firm would pay up to get me back — or maybe they just made a mistake and took me for somebody else."

He was a cool-headed liar and for the spur of the moment it was a good try. Yamamoto turned an enquiring glance in my direction and I shook my head sadly.

"This was no ordinary kidnap. Fujimara was a Chinese agent. The two men who planned your kidnapping were here tonight, and I believe they were planning the best method of shipping you into China. You would have been drugged again and bundled into a packing crate. Then a short trip by air, or by the next Chinese freighter to call at Osaka or Kobe. If we had not arrived, Mister Fallon, you would have been a very special delivery — destination Peking!"

Fallon's jaw dropped a few millimetres and he stopped fingering his sore wrists. He stared at me warily and then demanded:

"Why the hell should the Red Chinese want a nobody like me? And just who the hell are you, anyway?"

"Just answer the first question," Yamamoto suggested. "My curiosity has become overwhelming."

"Very well. I'll explain the whole pattern of events as I believe they must have happened. Some of the details still need confirmation, but it's the only way in which all the pieces fit logically together."

I smiled politely as I spoke and moved my position so that I was between Fallon and the doorway to the gardens. We were standing in a luxuriously carpeted corridor, lined on either side with expensive Japanese prints, and Yamamoto was blocking the way to the interior of the house.

"The story begins in Detroit, with an engineer named Richard Brett." I was watching Fallon's face and saw his mouth tighten. I continued confidently: "Brett developed a new type of battery for an electricity powered car. Something that could store energy out of all proportion to its size and make long range electric transport a commercial possibility. For most engineers that achievement in itself would have been enough, but Brett went one stage further. He designed a car with silicone body panels to convert solar energy into the electricity needed for the batteries. In an energy-starved world that is polluting itself to extinction Brett designed the free energy, pollution-free car of the future, the solar-electric car."

Yamamoto couldn't help himself. He blinked rapidly half a dozen times.

I stared grimly at Fallon. "Richard Brett was your friend. He took you into his confidence. That was his fatal mistake. Brett vanished from Detroit shortly before you left for Japan. Later his car was recovered from Lake Michigan with bloodstains inside. Perhaps you will eventually tell us how you killed him, and how you disposed of the body?"

Fallon didn't volunteer the information. He simply glared at me with his mouth set tight. He had forgotten his rope burns and his hands were knotted into fists at his sides.

I shrugged. "It doesn't matter. The fact remains that you killed Richard Brett and stole his notes, his designs, the battery formulae and all the results of his work. They would be worth a fortune to the right automobile company, perhaps they were beyond price. But you couldn't sell them in Detroit where too many people were aware of the general trend of Brett's research. If you had tried to pass his ideas off as your own in the city where you were both well known, then somebody would have remembered Brett's disappearance and started fitting the facts together."

Fallon denied nothing. He was visibly shaken. I looked past him to Yamamoto who was a fascinated listener.

"That's why Fallon came to Japan. He had connections in the car industry here, and he hoped that the Japanese wouldn't question his claim too closely. He visited the Koga car factory and offered the results of Brett's work to Shinjira."

I smiled faintly at a memory. "Shinjira is a devious man. He told me that Fallon had tried to sell him a new design which he suspected might be stolen, but he was careful to make it sound like an artist's sketch for a new style of the conventional petrol driven car. He hoped to mislead me if I ever got a scent of the truth elsewhere."

"So Mister Shinjira wanted the new ideas but he did not want to pay for them," Yamamoto suggested brightly. "Instead he paid the *Yakusa* to eliminate Mister Fallon?"

"It's more complicated than that," I answered ruefully. "What Fallon didn't know when he approached Shinjira, is that the Koga car company is a subsidiary of Osaka Oil, one of the biggest petroleum companies in Japan with a huge chain of petrol-filling stations throughout the far east. And Shinjira is on the board of directors with twenty-five percent share holdings in Osaka Oil. His interest was in the continued production of petrol driven cars. He didn't give a damn for the problems of energy-conservation and pollution. A feasible solar-electric car capturing the world markets would greatly benefit the world in general — but it would be a financial catastrophe for Shinjira and Osaka Oil."

Yamamoto nodded his understanding. Fallon was also beginning to understand where he had gone wrong and his face was bitter.

"Shinjira did employ the *Yakusa* to eliminate Fallon." I conceded Yamamoto's point. "No doubt there was a cash price, but Kukiko hinted once that he also played upon *Yakusa* loyalty to the lower paid workers who provide their support. Shinjira probably stressed the fact that a new car with a simplified power of motion would mean lost jobs for a vast number of car workers in the established industry. Either way, the *Yakusa* accepted the contract."

"The Chinese and Fujimara?" Yamamoto asked tentatively. He couldn't yet see how they fitted in.

"There was an industrial spy working inside Koga cars," I explained. "The girl Naoka, who was Shinjira's secretary. She had a habit of listening in to his business talks, She had already sold Koga secrets to rival car firms, including the details of a costly advertising campaign which Koga had to scrap. I'm certain she overheard Shinjira's conversation with Fallon. She knew what Fallon had to offer and she could see that this information could also be highly profitable. Her problem was to find the right market. She suspected that the solar-electric car might be equally unwelcome to all the other car companies with vast sums of money already invested in conventional car production. Finally she offered her information to a member of the Red Chinese trade delegation when they made their first visit to Koga cars."

"Of course!" Yamamoto's face was

an enlightened beam. "In Red China the main forms of transport are still the bicycle and the wheelbarrow. They desperately need a modern system of transportation. And in Red China there are no capitalist profiteers like Mister Shinjira to worry if the established automobile industry becomes obsolete."

I nodded agreement. "The Chinese saw the full potential of the solar-electric car. They decided that the discovery must be exploited by the People's Republic, which meant that Fallon had to be kidnapped and smuggled discreetly into China. Shang and Hu were the best men available for the job which had to be done quickly. They arranged it with Fujimara and Fallon was brought here."

"The girl was involved?" Yamamoto guessed.

"That's right. Naoka helped with the kidnapping. Later, when I appeared asking questions, she saw an opportunity for selling more information to the Chinese. If I was a threat she could warn them, and she expected to be well rewarded. Unfortunately she got over confident. She was making herself too obvious and so Shang and Hu murdered her."

I paused and then concluded, "The *Yakusa* were searching for Fallon all the time. They had accepted a contract to kill him and they intended to honour it. It would be a matter of face."

"Of course." Yamamoto understood all about face. He scratched his grey-bristled head for a moment and then looked at Fallon, his expression invited comment.

"I think this guy is nuts," Fallon said. "I've never heard of any guy called Richard Brett, in Detroit or anywhere else. And there's no such thing as a solar-electric car!"

I don't know how long Sharon Vale had been listening but she chose that precise moment to show herself and hurl a ringing challenge down the narrow hallway.

"You're a liar, Tony! You're a liar,

and a murderer, and a thief!"

Fallon's head jerked round at the familiar use of his name. Yamamoto turned more slowly. Sharon approached with the grim tread of an executioner. Her face was a brittle mask of bitterness, while her eyes burned with the bright blue flames of vengeance. In her right hand she held the Nambu 8 millimetre automatic.

I stepped between her and Fallon.

Sharon stopped.

"Stand aside, David. I hired you to find Fallon so that I could kill him — and I'm going to do it now. If you don't get out of my way I'll kill you too."

18

I DIDN'T move. Not because I thought Fallon was worth saving, but because I didn't want Sharon to make a mistake. She was still my client and I had a moral responsibility to at least give her the right advice. There was also the embarrassing fact that I had entrusted her with the gun. I hadn't expected this but I knew she had secrets. I had blundered badly and it was up to me to put matters right.

"Why, Sharon?" I asked her gently. I sensed that after all the pretence and deceit she wanted me to know, and it was possible that relief would ease her tension.

"Because I loved Richard Brett," she said in anguish. "Richard was my fiancé. He was the man I should have married. I warned him about Tony but he wouldn't listen. Poor, trusting Richard, he always tried to see the best in everybody. When he disappeared — and his file containing all his notes and designs — I knew Tony Fallon had to be responsible. I couldn't prove anything, but I didn't need to. I just promised myself I would find Tony and make him pay."

"And you needed the help of a gullible private detective," I said sadly. "Was I considered expendable right from the beginning? Did you plan to cover your tracks by killing me as soon as I had located Fallon?"

"No, David!" She was shocked and angered by the suggestion. "I don't care what happens to me. I just want to kill Tony." She made an impatient gesture with the automatic and added desperately: "But I will kill you if you stand in my way. I'm not going to be stopped."

"You are distraught," Yamamoto said hopefully. "Please give me the gun."

He held out his hand but she took

a step backwards.

"This is your last chance, David. I'll count to three."

She was serious, but mercifully she didn't begin to count. I had faintly heard the engines of another launch as it drew up to the jetty a few moments before, and our private drama was rudely interrupted by the arrival of the police reinforcements. They flooded the house, looking for Yamamoto, and thrusting ahead of the advance party was a young man who was obviously not Japanese. He wore horn-rimmed glasses and a bold black and white check sports jacket with grey slacks. He bounded down the hallway when he saw us and shouted Sharon's name.

She turned at the sound of his voice and her face went white. The Nambu slid from her suddenly nervous fingers and thudded on to the carpet. There was sheer disbelief in her eyes and an agony of longing. She took one faltering step forward and then fainted away into the encircling sweep of his outstretched arms.

I breathed a deep sigh of relief.

There was a familiar face among the new arrivals. Ken Kenichi strode up with a round beam of triumph.

"I found Robert Baxter for you, David," he explained cheerfully. "I also heard you were in bad trouble with the police, so I asked him to accompany me to Osaka. We called at Central Police Headquarters and they agreed we should come straight out to Kamajima."

"Thanks, Ken." I knew I owed him an apology. "But his name isn't Robert Baxter." I couldn't claim to have had an inspired flash of deduction because Sharon's reactions had made it all too obvious. "His real name is Richard Brett."

Yamamoto blinked on cue, while Kenichi looked faintly bewildered. Tony Fallon reflected the shocked horror of a man confronted with a ghost from the grave.

"You were dead," Fallon croaked.

"Not quite." Brett cradled Sharon in his arms, but his expression changed from one of concern to disgust as he looked up at his false friend. "You battered me about the head and spilled a lot of my blood, and you almost drowned me in the lake. I still don't know exactly how I survived. It was pouring with rain that night so the people who found me soaking wet on the lakeside road thought I'd been involved in an ordinary road accident. I was in a coma for a few days, but when I came out I let them carry on thinking the same thing. I didn't want you to be arrested before I was on my feet. When the police walked in on you I wanted to be right there beside them."

He paused bitterly. "The only trouble was, by the time I was well enough to move, you had skipped out to Japan. When I found Sharon had followed you I did the same."

Fallon swallowed hard but he had nothing to say. There was no more hope in bluff or denial so he tried the only course that was left. When I had stepped forward to confront Sharon I had left him a clear run to the open doorway to the gardens. Fallon spun on his heel and dived through it in a blind bid for freedom.

Yamamoto gave a bellow of anger and plunged in pursuit. I followed at his heels and behind me came Kenichi and a small pack of Japanese policemen and detectives.

Fallon was already disappearing fast through the cherry trees. The ragged clouds had moved to cover the stars and there was pitch darkness beneath the lush tangles of foliage.

It was a pity Yamamoto had got to the doorway first. With his figure he wasn't cut out to be a champion runner and he blocked the rest of us for a few vital seconds. By the time I had manoeuvred past him Fallon was lost from sight. I tried listening for the sounds of his escape, but with so many Japanese spreading out behind me and trampling down the shrubbery it was hopeless.

For a minute or two we milled about the gardens like stampeding sheep, dashing to and fro and bumping into each other in the general confusion. Yamamoto shouted orders and called up more men to the search. Then I heard a warning shout from the beach.

I headed in that direction fast. I was remembering suddenly that there had been a small motor boat tied up to the jetty.

As I reached the open sand Yamamoto appeared again at my side. We ran together and fifty yards ahead I saw Fallon as a dim outline crouched over the mooring line on the jetty. He cast off and jumped down into the boat. I was racing ahead of Yamamoto but I was still too late. Fallon succeeded in starting the boat's engine at the first attempt and headed out to sea.

I skidded to a frustrated stop, knowing I couldn't catch him.

Yamamoto blundered up beside me. He was breathing heavily and his police revolver was in his hand. He levelled it and aimed, and then fired one shot.

The bullet missed Fallon, but hit the steering wheel with spectacular results. The motor boat spun out of control in a leaping half circle turn, just as Fallon opened the throttle. He was thrown out over the side and his foot must have been entangled in the mooring rope. As the empty motor boat accelerated across the shallow bay Fallon was dragged helplessly in its creaming wake.

He was screaming and I remembered all those razor sharp oyster shells that littered the seabed. They had slashed through patent leather shoes to cripple Shino and his companions — and abruptly I decided that I didn't want to think about it any more.

A police launch moved out from the far end of the jetty to intercept the runaway motor boat, but by then the screaming had stopped.

I turned away and walked slowly up the beach. The clouds had drifted overhead and the stars were shining again. For the first time I noticed a red-lacquered *tori* gateway leading into the gardens. The scent of cherry blossom was caught up in the night breeze.

It was all very lovely, but right now I was prepared to swap it all for a very large scotch.

THE END

A FOOT IN THE GRAVE
Bruce Marshall

About to be imprisoned and tortured in Buenos Aires, John Smith escapes, only to become involved in an aeroplane hijacking.

DEAD TROUBLE
Martin Carroll

Trespassing brought Jennifer Denning more than she bargained for. She was totally unprepared for the violence which was to lie in her path.

HOURS TO KILL
Ursula Curtiss

Margaret went to New Mexico to look after her sick sister's rented house and felt a sharp edge of fear when the absent landlady arrived.

THE DEATH OF ABBE DIDIER
Richard Grayson

Inspector Gautier of the Sûreté investigates three crimes which are strangely connected.

NIGHTMARE TIME
Hugh Pentecost

Have the missing major and his wife met with foul play somewhere in the Beaumont Hotel, or is their disappearance a carefully planned step in an act of treason?

BLOOD WILL OUT
Margaret Carr

Why was the manor house so oddly familiar to Elinor Howard? Who would have guessed that a Sunday School outing could lead to murder?

THE DRACULA MURDERS
Philip Daniels

The Horror Ball was interrupted by a spectral figure who warned the merrymakers they were tampering with the unknown.

THE LADIES
OF LAMBTON GREEN
Liza Shepherd

Why did murdered Robin Colquhoun's picture pose such a threat to the ladies of Lambton Green?

CARNABY
AND THE GAOLBREAKERS
Peter N. Walker

Detective Sergeant James Aloysius Carnaby-King is sent to prison as bait. When he joins in an escape he is thrown headfirst into a vicious murder hunt.

MUD IN HIS EYE
Gerald Hammond

The harbourmaster's body is found mangled beneath Major Smyle's yacht. What is the sinister significance of the illicit oysters?

THE SCAVENGERS
Bill Knox

Among the masses of struggling fish in the *Tecta*'s nets was a larger, darker, ominously motionless form . . . the body of a skin diver.

DEATH IN ARCADY
Stella Phillips

Detective Inspector Matthew Furnival works unofficially with the local police when a brutal murder takes place in a caravan camp.

STORM CENTRE
Douglas Clark

Detective Chief Superintendent Masters, temporarily lecturing in a police staff college, finds there's more to the job than a few weeks relaxation in a rural setting.

THE MANUSCRIPT MURDERS
Roy Harley Lewis

Antiquarian bookseller Matthew Coll, acquires a rare 16th century manuscript. But when the Dutch professor who had discovered the journal is murdered, Coll begins to doubt its authenticity.

SHARENDEL
Margaret Carr

Ruth didn't want all that money. And she didn't want Aunt Cass to die. But at Sharendel things looked different. She began to wonder if she had a split personality.

MURDER TO BURN
Laurie Mantell

Sergeants Steven Arrow and Lance Brendon, of the New Zealand police force, come upon a woman's body in the water. When the dead woman is identified they begin to realise that they are investigating a complex fraud.

YOU CAN HELP ME
Maisie Birmingham

Whilst running the Citizens' Advice Bureau, Kate Weatherley is attacked with no apparent motive. Then the body of one of her clients is found in her room.

DAGGERS DRAWN
Margaret Carr

Stacey Manston was the kind of girl who could take most things in her stride, but three murders were something different . . .

THE MONTMARTRE MURDERS
Richard Grayson

Inspector Gautier of Sûreté investigates the disappearance of artist Théo, the heir to a fortune.

GRIZZLY TRAIL
Gwen Moffat

Miss Pink, alone in the Rockies, helps in a search for missing hikers, solves two cruel murders and has the most terrifying experience of her life when she meets a grizzly bear!

BLINDMAN'S BLUFF
Margaret Carr

Kate Deverill had considered suicide. It was one way out — and preferable to being murdered.

BEGOTTEN MURDER
Martin Carroll

When Susan Phillips joined her aunt on a voyage of 12,000 miles from her home in Melbourne, she little knew their arrival would germinate the seeds of murder planted long ago.

WHO'S THE TARGET?
Margaret Carr

Three people whom Abby could identify as her parents' murderers wanted her dead, but she decided that maybe Jason could have been the target.

THE LOOSE SCREW
Gerald Hammond

After a motor smash, Beau Pepys and his cousin Jacqueline, her fiancé and dotty mother, suspect that someone had prearranged the death of their friend. But who, and why?

CASE WITH THREE HUSBANDS
Margaret Erskine

Was it a ghost of one of Rose Bonner's late husbands that gave her old Aunt Agatha such a terrible shock and then murdered her in her bed?

THE END OF THE RUNNING
Alan Evans

Lang continued to push the men and children on and on. Behind them were the men who were hunting them down, waiting for the first signs of exhaustion before they pounced.

CARNABY AND THE HIJACKERS
Peter N. Walker

When Commander Pigeon assigns Detective Sergeant Carnaby-King to prevent a raid on a bullion-carrying passenger train, he knows that there are traitors in high positions.

TREAD WARILY AT MIDNIGHT
Margaret Carr

If Joanna Morse hadn't been so hasty she wouldn't have been involved in the accident.

TOO BEAUTIFUL TO DIE
Martin Carroll

There was a grave in the churchyard to prove Elizabeth Weston was dead. Alive, she presented a problem. Dead, she could be forgotten. Then, in the eighth year of her death she came back. She was beautiful, but she had to die.

IN COLD PURSUIT
Ursula Curtiss

In Mexico, Mary and her cousin Jenny each encounter strange men, but neither of them realises that one of these men is obsessed with revenge and murder. But which one?

LITTLE DROPS OF BLOOD
Bill Knox

It might have been just another unfortunate road accident but a few little drops of blood pointed to murder.

GOSSIP TO THE GRAVE
Jonathan Burke

Jenny Clark invented Simon Sherborne because her daily gossip column was getting dull. Then Simon appeared at a party — in the flesh! And Jenny finds herself involved in murder.

HARRIET FAREWELL
Margaret Erskine

Wealthy Theodore Buckler had planned a magnificent Guy Fawkes Day celebration. He hadn't planned on murder.

SANCTUARY ISLE
Bill Knox

Chief Detective Inspector Colin Thane and Detective Inspector Phil Moss are sent to a bird sanctuary off the coast of Argyll to investigate the murder of the warden.

THE SNOW ON THE BEN
Ian Stuart

Although on holiday in the Highlands, Chief Inspector Hamish MacLeod begins an investigation when a pistol shot shatters the quiet of his solitary morning walk.

HARD CONTRACT
Basil Copper

Private detective Mike Farraday is hired to obtain settlement of a debt from Minsky. But Minsky is killed before Mike can get to him. A spate of murders follows.

VICIOUS CIRCLE
Alan Evans

Crawford finds himself on the run and hunted in a strange land, wanting only to find his son but prepared to pay any cost.

DEATH ON A QUIET BEACH
Simon Challis

For Thurston, the blonde on the beach was routine. Within hours he had another body to deal with, and suddenly it wasn't routine any more.

DEATH IN THE SCILLIES
Howard Charles Davis

What had happened to the yachtsman whose boat had drifted on to the Seven Sisters Reef? Who is recruiting a bodyguard for a millionaire and why should bodyguards be needed in the Scillies.